Befallen

LOVE ALL ELSE BOOK ONE

SHIRLEY SIATON

Inky Sword Book Publishing

ISBN 978-1-961052-38-3

1st Edition, July 2025 (The Eternal Flame Edition)

Published by Shirley S. Parabia

Cover design by Xielle Graphics

Barangay Quezon, Arevalo, Iloilo City 5000 Philippines

Content Warnings

Warnings for mild profanity, acts of violence, and content of an explicit nature.

Recommended for mature readers 18 years old and above.

Playlist

A Thousand Years ~ Christina Perri

Rewrite the Stars ~ Anne-Marie & James Arthur

Here With Me ~ Dido

Iris ~ Goo Goo Dolls

It's All Coming Back to Me Now ~ Marion Raven & Meat Loaf

Can You Die From a Broken Heart ~ Avril Lavigne & Nate Smith

My Immortal ~ Evanescence

To Peter

Whom I will love
until all the stars die

Contents

Prologue

THE ETERNAL SKIES

I will not live forever.

Life is but a flicker in the eternal skies.

It is a truth, even for my kind. Even the legends speak of this transience.

I still remember, dimly, the days before the war, when we listened to our elders around the quiet crackle of fire burning in the deepest roots. The tales spoke of towering branches reaching the clouds, paths lined with fragrant blooms, and endless verdant fields where we could run without fear.

I listened then, and wondered.

That was hundreds of sun-cycles ago. I grew up in a world

where war was inevitable. I prepared for it. I was ready when it came through the delicate veil of water and earth.

I fought. For so long.

But will I live long enough to see its end?

It does not matter. I will start its end, one way or another.

The night is cold and wet when I cross the veil.

Rain falls in sheets, soft but endless, as if the sky is mourning something it cannot name. The new moon hides itself behind thick clouds, cloaking everything in deeper shadow, but the raindrops still shimmer faintly, silver threads in the dark.

My feet sink into unfamiliar ground, softer and colder than what I am used to. The world on this side feels thinner, quieter.

My body is broken. Torn. The wound in my side still leaks warmth I cannot afford to lose. I press a hand to it as I stagger forward.

I should not be alive, but I am.

Because of the ember.

The very thing I stole back from them. The thing they bled me for. Fought me for. Killed for.

I thought I could contain it. I was wrong.

It did not just save me.

It claimed me.

Now, it pulses beneath my ribs. I can feel it flickering through my veins like a second heartbeat. It does not belong to this world, or the one I left.

And neither do I. Not anymore.

My eyes adjust quickly, warily. The ember in me, the only light I have left, guides my steps. Its glow is faint, hidden beneath skin and scar, but it is there. Burning.

I do not know where I have landed.

I do not know if this world is safer than the one I left behind.

But I walk anyway, because there is no going back.

The rain is a mercy. The blood streaming from my body washes away before it can stain the ground. No one will see my weakness.

The earth beneath me is slippery and treacherous, but I do not falter. I am the First Commander of the High Crown. It will take more than water or wind to bring me to my knees.

Then I see it.

In a clearing at the end of the muddy path, something small stands in the shifting glow of fireflies. The soft golden lights drift and swirl, defying the rain.

The figure before me is too tiny to be someone who has crossed over, too frail to be anything other than...

A two-legged creature. Upright on tiny legs.

I stumble toward it, one hand outstretched, grasping at what can only be hope—or death.

"I want to go home." A hesitant voice cuts through the softly howling wind. "I was looking for *datiles*, but it got dark quickly so I followed the fireflies. Will you take me home, sir?"

The flickering light falls onto the rounded face of a human child. Wide eyes, tiny nose, trembling lips.

A female. Delicate. Young. No more than a few sun-cycles old.

She can see me.

But that is not what astonishes me the most.

There is no fear.

I know fear intimately. I have endured it, fought against it, tasted it on the breath and blood of my enemies. This child has none.

"Shelter," I croak out. I know the tongue of their world, well enough to speak it. My footing wavers. The woods around me sway like leaves in the breeze. *"I need to find shelter."*

"Shelter?" The child repeats the word, unmoving. "I don't know...I'm lost. Are you lost too?"

"Yes...I am lost, too, little one."

She hesitates, then takes a step closer. The top of her head barely reaches my waist. It has been so long since I have seen a human child.

"Can we get lost together?" she asks. "You look very strong. I don't think I'll be scared if you're lost with me."

Her tiny hand reaches out, fingers wrapping around my thumb, stark white against the dark of my flesh.

I open my mouth, but no words come. In that moment, she looks up, up, up.

Into my eyes.

Her gaze is a deep pool of starless midnight, where the sun sleeps in the arms of the moon. And in it, I see...

The eternal skies.

A babe, giggling and cooing.

A child, sneaking away to forage for datiles *in the woods.*

A woman, running in the rain, into my arms.

The stab wounds in my body are nothing compared to the pain of the visions.

My hand falls away from hers. The earth trembles. The roots of the forever tree break through the soil, wrapping around me like chains, pulling me toward where she was, is, and will be. Lightning shatters the sky. Thunder roars. The world tears itself apart.

And I, the First Commander of the High Crown, fall to my knees.

I do not know how long I remain that way, my body anchoring me to the ground, my heart, fingertips, and eyes burning with the hottest, whitest flames. My own cry of agony shakes the forest.

An eternity passes before the rain thins to a drizzle and the wind calms its heart. Only then do I open my eyes.

My hands are buried in the dirt. It takes all my strength to lift my head.

She is kneeling before me. Her small hands rest on my chest, her fingers disappearing into the dark curls of hair.

A sense of triumph and wonder swells in me, despite the pain.

She is the first to speak. Her voice is a cool breeze in the damp night. "Are you okay? Are you hurt?"

I shake my head, trying to swallow the heat and cold, the bitter and sweet rising in my throat.

I look into her eyes.

All the sun-cycles and moon-rises before and after this moment no longer matter.

It is she.

I am hers.

My fingers graze her hair, my thumb brushing her cheek. A soft growl rumbles from my chest as I find my voice again, as I remember the words of the humans.

"I will get lost with you."

Chapter 1

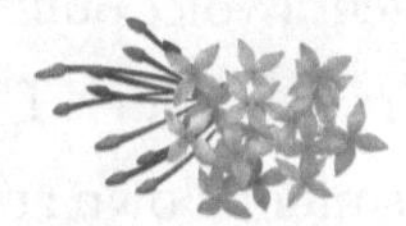

The Rain that Fell

HELENA

Home.

I don't think I ever really understood what that word meant until a few months ago.

Not the city. Not the pretty off-white suburban house with its glass windows or the high-rise apartment with a pool overlooking the river. Not the places where my parents built their lives, expecting me to fit neatly inside them.

No, home is here.

Concepcion.

After all these years, after everything that's happened, I know it now. I feel it in my bones, in the way the air fills my lungs a little differently here. I should have never left. I should have grown up on these roads, under this sun, next to my grandparents instead of in a city where I never truly belonged.

But there's no undoing the past. There's only this moment. And right now, home is waiting.

"Miss, excuse me?" A gentle voice pulls me from my thoughts, a light hand squeezing my shoulder. I blink up at Josie, the conductor's wife, who's smiling down at me. "We've arrived."

I sit up, stretching my stiff limbs. Outside the window, the landscape is painfully familiar. The green and brown rice fields stretch toward the hills on the horizon, golden in the late afternoon sun. It rained earlier, but the world now glows in that soft, hazy way it does before dusk.

"It's been so long," I say softly. "I forgot how beautiful it is."

Josie nods. "Rey and I will help with your things."

I shake my head and sling my backpack over one shoulder. "No, it's okay. Thank you."

As I make my way to the front of the bus, I catch sight of the three other passengers, all glued to their phones, barely noticing the stop. I say a quick goodbye to the driver before stepping onto the pavement. My duffel bag is already on the side of the road, waiting.

Rey, the conductor, grins at me. "I bet your grandparents are excited to have you home. Are you staying until the end of summer?"

"Maybe longer," I say.

Josie joins him. "Our daughter's starting college in the city. You're gonna be a junior at the university, right?"

I hesitate. "I'm...not sure yet," I finally answer. "I'll find out soon."

I don't give them time to ask more. Instead, I pull out my phone, gathering them for a quick selfie before they head off. I watch the bus pull away, disappearing down the road, leaving only the sound of the wind and the rustling fields.

When I check my phone, I have four unread messages. I move to the waiting shed and sit on the concrete bench before checking them. One from Janine, one from my mother, one from Lola, and—

I press my lips together and delete the last one without opening it.

> *Where did u go? I called*

It's all I glimpse on the preview before my fingers press the *Delete* button.

It doesn't matter.

I open my grandmother's message. It's a voice note, sent an hour ago. Her warm, familiar voice spills through the speaker.

"Hi, sweetheart. I'm so sorry for doing this at the last minute. I tried calling, but your phone was out of range. Lolo had an asthma attack after lunch, so we're at the hospital for some tests. He's okay now. Tomas will pick you up. I can't recall if I told you about him, but he's been helping us out at home. I'll give him this phone so he can call you. We love you. We'll see you tonight."

I play the message again. *Tomas.* I don't remember her mentioning him much. I assumed he was one of the local boys my grandparents always hired for odd jobs.

They liked having kids around. I always suspected it was

because of me, because I wasn't there. Lola used to show me their pictures on her phone whenever she and Lolo visited us in the city.

I hated it. I hated knowing they had other children keeping them company. Children from the village climbing coconut trees, harvesting vegetables, and helping Lola in the garden. On special occasions, they gather in the kitchen, rolling out dough for *empanada* or helping Lolo tie up ducks to make *patotim* for the village *fiesta*.

I should have been in those pictures. I should have been the one beside them, laughing, working, belonging. Not those other kids.

Looking back, no amount of party selfies or perfectly curated OOTD posts can replace the memories I never had the chance to make with the people I love the most.

But there's no room or time for regrets now.

I shake it off, answering my mother first with a quick text. I don't tell her about Lolo's asthma. I'll tell her later, when I know more.

I text Janine back, letting her know I'm just waiting for my ride to the house.

I miss her.

Right now, she's probably buried in student council work, juggling meetings and color-coded spreadsheets, planning the perfect events for freshmen and returning students, every detail honed by her laser focus and impossible standards. She loves this time of year. She thrives in it. I used to love being part of it with her.

Used to.

I can picture her even now. She'd be on the steps of the administration building, phone tucked between her ear and shoulder, snapping orders and smiling in that way that makes people say yes without thinking. She was always the hurricane. I was the anchor. We were the perfect team.

Until I let go.

And now, I'm not beside her. Not when she needs someone to design and set up the welcome booths in the scorching heat, or call her out when she forgets to eat.

I wish I could be there with her, helping her pick the perfect dress for the acquaintance party, the biggest event at the start of the new school year. I can already hear her voice as she holds up options in front of the mirror, demanding brutal honesty and nothing less.

She never needed help turning heads. But it became our thing, ever since I was thirteen and somehow ended up walking for a local designer's line. That was the moment I became Ellie, the teen fashion queen of Iloilo—whether I liked it or not.

The clock app reads 4:07 PM. No sign of Tomas. Maybe he got distracted. If he's a teenage boy, that wouldn't be surprising.

I debate whether to call my grandparents again, just to let them know where I am. But I don't want to bother them, not with Lolo's condition. Besides, I'm in no rush. I might as well make the most of this time.

I set my backpack down beside my duffel bag and stand, smoothing out my clothes. Just a simple blouse and jeans, light and easy for travel but decent enough for photos. Back in the city, I was known for my cute dresses.

Was known.

I step out of the shed and open the front camera on my phone, adjusting the lighting. I used to be good at this. There was a time when no one else could do better at angles and filters, at getting the perfect shot. I got those sponsors for a reason, after all.

I snap a few selfies with the rice fields in the background, the golden light hitting just right.

Then, just as I press the button once more, a shadow moves into my frame, blocking the view.

I frown and look up.

A man stands across the narrow road, next to a motorcycle. He's tall. Taller than most. He wears a checkered gray shirt over dark trousers, his long black hair pulled back, some strands loose around his face. He's holding a phone to his ear, his gaze locked onto me.

My phone begins to ring. Lola's number flashes on the screen.

I swipe to answer. "Hello?"

A deep, unfamiliar voice comes through. "Is this Miss Helena?"

"Who's this?"

"My name is Tomas. Your grandparents sent me."

Slowly, I lower my phone and meet his eyes.

Brown. But not just brown. A strange, light shade, catching the sunlight in a way I don't understand.

He watches me closely. A little too closely.

I lift a hand hesitantly. If I'm wrong, I'll just apologize and move on. But he nods, pockets his phone, and walks toward me.

The closer he gets, the more I realize I can't look away.

He moves gracefully for someone his size. His features are angular, his brows thick, his eyes deep-set, shadowed beneath long lashes. The late afternoon light catches on the fine lines of muscle beneath his shirt, hinting at a body built from labor.

He looks...familiar. But I can't place why.

He stops a respectful distance away, holding out a hand. He moves quietly, as if he doesn't want any attention. "I'm Tomas."

I take it. His palm is warm. Larger than mine. Rough, like someone who works with his hands.

"Helena." It feels strange to introduce myself by my given name. I've been 'Ellie' for so long that I almost forget what my real name sounds like. "Just Helena, please."

His brown eyes flicker at the sound of my name. My face somehow feels warmer in response.

No, gold.

His eyes are almost gold, in the right light.

"I'm sorry I'm late," he says, lowering his gaze. "The motorcycle ran out of fuel on the way here. Lolo Emil doesn't use it as often anymore."

"It's fine," I say. "I'm not in a hurry. Thanks for coming."

He shakes his head a bit. "I'm really sorry."

I can't help but smile. Straightforward apologies are rare in the city. "It's not a big deal. Please stop apologizing. It's fine, really."

He looks a little flustered, stepping around me before nodding toward my sparse luggage on the waiting shed bench. "Are these all your things?"

I nod. "Yes."

He picks up both my bags with one hand. "Lola said you wouldn't be bringing much, so they made me take the motorcycle. They were both really worried they couldn't pick you up."

I follow him to the motorcycle, recognizing it instantly. It's the Honda my father bought for my grandfather's birthday a few years ago. "And Lolo? How is he?"

Tomas ties my bags to the back, his hands moving quickly and efficiently. "He's fine. He just had to take some medicine to feel better. This happened last month too. I think that's why the doctor made him go to the hospital."

The familiarity in the way he talks about my grandparents doesn't escape me. "How long have you been working for Lolo and Lola?"

"Almost a year," he says, handing me a helmet. "They've been very kind to me."

It hits me, for the first time, that I actually have to ride with him.

"Wait." I take the helmet but set it aside on the motorcycle seat, switching on my phone's camera. "Let's take a picture first."

I sidle up beside him, holding the phone up for a selfie, angling it just right. Standing on my toes, I manage to fit both our faces in the frame. He looks utterly bewildered in the photo, like someone who's never taken a selfie before.

He waits patiently, silently, as I send the picture to my grandfather, along with a quick message.

By the time I finish, I look up and find him holding out the polo shirt he had on. Beneath it, he's wearing a plain black t-shirt.

"This should give you some cover in case it rains," he says. "It might rain again."

Most of the guys I know wouldn't think to do something like this. They're more likely to take off your clothes than give you theirs.

"Thanks, but you don't have to. I'll be fine if it rains."

He only shakes his head.

There's something so undeniably sincere about him, making it hard to argue. I tuck my phone into my handbag and slip the shirt on, leaving it unbuttoned and tying it loosely around my waist.

"I'll make sure you get a clean raincoat first thing in the morning," he adds, securing his helmet. "Lolo has some, but they're all dirty. It's been raining almost every day for weeks now."

Again, the way he speaks about my grandparents makes me wonder just how close he really is to them.

"Thanks," I say, putting on my helmet.

He swings a leg over the motorcycle and inclines his head for me to do the same.

And now it's my turn to feel flustered. It's been months since I've been this close to a boy—since I broke up with my ex. And Tomas...I barely know him. Yet here I am, supposed to put my arms around him.

"I was ten the last time I rode a motorcycle," I admit. "I hope I don't fall off or anything."

"I won't let anything happen to you," he says solemnly. "It's my job to look after you, Helena."

I hope I'm not blushing as I carefully swing my leg over the bike, easing into the seat behind him.

The warmth of his body seeps into mine. He smells like soap and something woodsy, like fresh morning dew and the deep, earthy scent of trees.

I miss the woods. I miss them so much it hurts. I still remember the countless hours I spent there before I left for the city.

"Are you ready to go?" he asks.

I wrap my arms around his waist, feeling the solid warmth of him beneath my touch. I can feel his breath, steady and even. I can feel my own breath, pressing against his back.

"Yes," I say softly. "Please take me home."

Chapter 2

The Road Home

TOMAS

I feel her before she even touches me.

Helena hesitates. Just for a second. But then her arms wrap around me, her fingers pressing through the thin fabric of my shirt as she settles onto the motorcycle. Her scent curls into my lungs. She smells of fresh petals, a little sweet and a little wild.

She is too close. Too warm.

I grip the handlebars harder than I should. I need to focus. The engine hums beneath us, the vibrations climbing through my body, through hers. I feel everything. Every breath she takes, every small movement of her body against mine. Her thighs press lightly against me. If I were a better man, I would not notice.

But I am not a better man.

She was once a child, small and curious, reckless in the way only children are. She used to run barefoot through the forest, collecting *datiles* in the skirt of her dress, dirt smeared across her cheeks. She used to laugh.

Now, she is a woman.

The road stretches ahead, winding and empty, the golden glow of the afternoon sun washing over the rice fields. The air is thick with the scent of damp earth, of burning leaves from nearby homes. The village of Santo Tomas has always been quiet, but tonight, it is too quiet. Or maybe it is just her.

I can barely hear her sigh over the sound of the wind rushing past us.

But then, she moves.

Her chest presses flush against my back, the curve of her body molding into mine as if she has always belonged there.

I feel my body lock up. My breathing slows. My hands tighten around the grips.

She is not doing it on purpose, I tell myself. She has not been on a bike for a while. She is just holding on, making sure she is safe.

She cannot know what she is doing to me. I am supposed to be in control. I have spent years in control. Years watching and waiting from a distance.

But now she is here. And she is touching me.

A small sound escapes her lips, a soft gasp as the bike takes a bump in the road. Her fingers twitch against my stomach, tightening ever so slightly.

I feel the moment I lose control.

Not much, just a fraction of a second where I let myself feel it, where I let the hunger coil in my stomach. It simmers, dangerously close to boiling over.

I swallow, pushing down the need, the ache, the fire in my blood. I turn my attention to the road. I do not let myself think of what would happen if I turned the bike around and kept driving.

The path is uneven beneath the tires, grooved and sticky from the earlier rain, with patches of loose gravel crunching under the weight of the motorcycle. Dust swirls behind us, catching the light as we pass. The village square is alive with the bustle of late-day routines. Children run across the packed dirt, their laughter ringing in the warm afternoon air, some pausing to wave as we speed by.

The *barangay* hall sits at the heart of it all, its sun-faded blue walls covered in posters. Beside it, the chapel stands open and inviting, its wooden doors propped wide, white walls still bright from the fresh coat of paint it received before the last *Flores de Mayo*.

The chapel is the first thing I remember of this village. The first place I was in.

The place I was *found* in.

Clusters of houses line the road. Some are built of bamboo and *nipa* palm, raised on stilts, while others are small cement homes with tin roofs. Smoke rises from backyard kitchens, carrying the scent of evening meals. We pass the school, its green-painted walls shaded by towering acacia trees.

Helena holds onto me, her arms snug around my waist. I can

feel the rise and fall of her breath, her presence anchoring me in a way I cannot fully grasp. The scent of her mixes with the earth, the fields, the smells of this place she has always belonged to.

By the time we reach the house, my head is spinning, but I tell myself, I cannot lose control. Not now. Not so soon.

I stop the bike, killing the engine. Neither of us moves. Neither of us speaks.

And then I notice.

Her fingers do not move from me.

Too long.

A second too long. Two. Three.

I breathe out, before I lift my hand and place it lightly over hers.

She freezes.

I know, right away, I made a mistake

A second too much. A touch too lingering. A silence too loaded.

So I let go.

I dismount before I can do something worse, something I cannot take back. She watches me, her eyes wide, her throat working as she swallows. I do not meet her gaze. If I do, I will not be able to look away.

"We're here," I say, my voice rougher than intended. "Welcome home."

She takes a second to move, but when she does, her legs are unsteady. I should not notice that. But I do.

I notice everything.

The way her skin glows, golden from the sun, smooth and soft, untouched by the roughness of this place. Her waist is small, delicate beneath the fabric of her clothes, but her curves are full, shapely, meant to be held.

I grab her bags before she can say anything, throwing the straps over my shoulder.

"I can—"

"I've got it." My voice is final. No room for argument. No room to linger and keep staring at her.

I push the gate to the main house, stepping into the front yard before she does. This place is mine, in a way not even *they* know. I know every creaking wooden step, every tree branch, every stone in the soil. I have spent years here, carving myself into its bones.

But Helena...she is what it was waiting for.

The Dosado farm is old, tiny but comfortable, lived-in, breathing with the weight of time. A wooden house with cream-colored walls, its paint peeling in places, mango trees stretching toward the sky, their fruit-heavy branches swaying with the wind. Rows upon rows of vegetables, rotated by season. A small rose garden, its delicate petals tended to with the same care as the home itself.

But it is the *santan* flowers that surround the house that always stand out. They grow in lush clusters of red, orange, and yellow blooms, like flames licking the edges of the walls.

I unlock the front door, holding it open for her. She walks into the house, her eyes taking in the details. Her gaze sweeps over the shelves, the wooden chairs and table, the curtains. It is all hers, even if she does not remember it.

The walls are lined with photographs of her as a child. Helena dressed in a white gown for *Santacruzan,* Helena with her grandparents, Helena holding baskets of mangoes, and many others.

She does not say anything, but I see the way her throat moves, the way her fingers flex at her sides.

"You must be hungry," I say. "I'll make something."

She looks in my direction, blinking rapidly, as if realizing she is not alone. "You cook?"

I nod. "Your grandparents like it when I help."

Her expression softens. And then something flickers in her eyes, something quiet and buried. Something that still aches.

I know what it is.

She has been gone too long. She has missed too much.

I know this feeling of time lost, intimately.

"Thank you," she says softly.

I nod once, but I do not leave. I do not want to.

I linger, watching her as she looks around, as she presses a hand to the wooden table, smiling down at a photograph of herself as a little girl showing off a handful of *datiles*.

I turn away, setting her bags down near the staircase that leads up to the bedrooms.

"Where are you from, Tomas? Are you from Concepcion?"

The questions catch me off guard.

I glance at her, but she is already looking at me intently. Her large brown eyes are focused despite the lightness in her voice, scanning my face, seemingly searching for something familiar.

No one looks at me like that. No one ever has.

"No," I say. "From somewhere else, I think. But...I don't remember."

Her brows pull together. "You don't remember?"

I shake my head, wondering what she thinks of me now. "Lolo

Emil found me in the chapel almost a year ago...and took me in. I was very sick."

"Did he?"

Something about the way she says it makes my chest tighten.

She tilts her head, still watching me. "I was pretty sure we've met before."

A strange feeling coils in my stomach.

"You haven't visited Iloilo, have you?" she presses, a teasing lilt to her voice. "Attended a party, maybe?"

"A party?"

She smirks. "Yeah, you look like someone who could have slipped into one of my after-hours events. You know, dim lights, a rooftop bar, music loud enough to feel in your chest. The kind of party where no one's really paying attention. Except when they are."

I shake my head. "A party like that? I don't think so."

She smiles a little. "Mmm. You wouldn't have been in the crowd, though. You'd be the guy standing in the corner, watching everything." Her eyes flick over me, deliberately. "Waiting."

"Waiting for what?" I ask.

"I don't know," she answers. "You tell me."

I shrug. "Probably you."

Helena's lips part slightly, her breath catching.

She hesitates at first.

Then she grips the hem of my polo shirt—the one I lent her earlier, the one she has been wearing over her own clothes.

And in one slow, fluid motion, she slides it off her shoulders.

The shirt peels away, revealing the soft curve of her shoulders, the gentle dip of her collarbone, the way her white top clings to her beneath it.

I stop breathing.

She does not rush. She knows exactly what she is doing.

The collar catches on her hair, making her shake her head to free it. The strands fall in soft, loose waves over her shoulders, some settling over her cheek, over the column of her throat, framing her face in a way that makes my pulse thunder in my ears.

She holds out the shirt between us, the fabric bunched in her hands. "Thanks for letting me borrow this, by the way."

I should just take it, then step back.

Instead, I reach for her.

Not for the shirt.

For her.

I lift my hand, slowly, and tuck a loose strand of hair behind her ear. My fingers graze the soft skin of her cheek. Her skin feels warm, like something kissed by the sun.

She stills.

I should stop.

But I do not. My touch lingers, tracing lightly down the curve of her jaw before falling away.

Her grip on the shirt tightens. For a second, she looks at me as if she wants something, daring me to take another step closer to find out what it is.

And for a second, I almost do.

And then—

We both turn toward the gate just as the tricycle sputters to a stop, its engine coughing before falling silent. For a few moments, there is only the rustling of the mango trees, the distant hum of cicadas, and the faint voices of the driver and passengers.

There's movement, muffled footfalls on the dirt outside.

Helena moves first, shoving the shirt into my hands. I see the way she stills for half a second, gathering herself, as if bracing for impact. Then she pushes open the door, moving onto the porch.

Otel Dosado is a few steps ahead of her husband, adjusting the woven basket in her arms. I already know she has bananas inside, for her fritters that she sells to the children at the elementary school. Every morning, the scent of fried sugar always fills the house before the sun even rises.

"Lola," Helena says shakily, rushing down the steps to meet her grandmother halfway.

Otel, who usually carries herself with the quiet dignity of a former schoolteacher, responds in kind, dropping her basket to the ground to pull Helena into her arms.

"*Apo*," she breathes thickly. "You're home. Finally."

I barely realize I am moving until I am already there, stepping past them, bending down to retrieve the fallen basket.

Helena buries her face in her grandmother's shoulder. "I missed you."

Otel's hands cup Helena's face when they pull apart. "You're still my beautiful girl. No matter how long you've been away."

Helena breathes out slowly, shaking her head. "Lola..."

"We're all here," Otel says, smoothing a stray strand of hair away from her face. "You need anything, you have us now. You have Tomas too."

My name lingers in the space between them.

, I stay still, my hands digging into the handle of the basket.

Emil joins them, his voice warm but laced with apology. "Helena, we're sorry we couldn't pick you up ourselves. The doctor wanted to run extra tests. Just routine, but we couldn't leave until they were done."

He is elderly and slightly stooped, but his steady, grounding presence fills the air with unspoken command. He is the man who took me in when I had nowhere to go. The man who, despite his years, still carries himself like someone who refuses to be beaten down by time. Once the number-one councilor of the Municipality of Concepcion, he still looks after his people as an official of the village of Santo Tomas.

He was the one who gave me my name, because I did not have one.

Helena shakes her head. "Lolo, you don't have to explain. I understand. Your health is more important. I can always find my way around."

Otel sighs, giving Emil a pointed look before turning back to Helena. "He had another asthma attack today, following last month's. They're getting worse. The doctor changed his medication and told him to rest more."

"It wasn't that bad," Emil mutters, but Otel silences him with a glare.

Helena's face tightens. "Lolo, you have to take it seriously. The farm isn't going anywhere. Please don't overwork yourself."

He chuckles. "That's what Tomas keeps telling me."

The mention of my name makes Helena glance at me.

Emil clears his throat. "Tomas, everything went okay when you picked her up?"

I nod. "Yes, sir. The bus was on time. No problems."

I wait for Helena to mention that I was late, but she only looks at me, her face unreadable.

Emil studies me for a beat before nodding. "Good. Good." Then he turns back to Helena, finally pulling her into his arms.

She stiffens for just a moment before melting into the embrace, gripping the back of his shirt. Emil holds her tightly, his hand settling on her shoulder before brushing down her back in a familiar, comforting motion. He does not say anything, but I see the moment he notices—the slight tremor in his grip, the way his fingers linger as if feeling for something that is no longer there.

Otel seems to notice it too. "Are your parents still following that keto nonsense they were talking about last time?"

Before Helena can answer, Emil presses a firm kiss to the top of her head before letting her go. "In that case, you must be hungry. Dinner will be ready soon."

Helena smiles. "I am."

"Good," he says, squeezing her shoulder before stepping back. "You need to eat more. You're back home now. No more city food, just your Lola's cooking. You're too thin."

A small laugh escapes her, though there is something fragile in it. "You've been saying that since I was fifteen, Lolo."

"And I'll keep saying it," he replies.

Then Emil claps me on the back, his expression warm and fatherly. "Tomas already knows what to do. He's been taking good care of us."

I do not need to be told.

Without a word, I step into the house, toward the kitchen, and begin preparing the food.

I know where everything is.

I do not have to ask.

Outside, the sun is dipping lower, casting golden light over the farm, over the mango trees heavy with fruit, over the neat rows of *ampalaya*, eggplant, *sitaw*, and tomatoes growing in the soil.

The place smells like earth.

Like home.

Chapter 3

The Midnight Lights

HELENA

The house smells like warm rice, fried fish, and the lingering sweetness of mangoes.

The floors still creak beneath my bare feet when I walk around, just like they used to when I was a child running from room to room, the wood worn smooth by time and love.

It is small, but every inch is familiar—my grandmother's old sewing machine in the corner, the small altar with a statue of the Virgin Mary surrounded by candles, the faded lace curtains fluttering against the warm evening air.

It feels like home. And yet, I am a stranger here.

Tomas had excused himself from dinner earlier, leaving Lola, Lolo, and me to talk among ourselves.

Lola Otel insists I sit and eat more than I can stomach.

"You're so thin, *apo*. You used to have such chubby cheeks." She pinches the air where my face used to be fuller.

Lolo Emil watches me with a careful gaze, his hands wrapped around his cup of coffee. There is a question in his eyes, one he does not ask outright.

"So, are you going back?" he asks finally.

I know what he means. University. My parents. My friends. The life I left behind in the city.

"I don't think so, Lolo."

Silence settles over the table. I feel Lola's eyes on me. She already knows my answer. She has always known, since that phone call last month, when I asked them if I could come home for the summer.

"It's not because of..." She doesn't finish. She doesn't have to.

I nod. "It is. I just want to be here, Lola."

It's the truth. Mostly.

But it's not the ultimate reason.

Lola reaches for my hand, her grip tightening as her eyes fill with tears. "Oh, *apo*. Can't they—"

I shake my head, interrupting her smoothly as I squeeze her hand back. "I missed this place. I missed you both."

Lolo nods slowly. "You always loved it here."

I glance around, at the pictures lining the walls. Their Helena. Their shining light. A life preserved in still frames.

I was born in Concepcion. I stayed with my grandparents when my parents decided to seek their fortune in Saudi Arabia when I was barely a year old.

I should have never left.

Lola nods vigorously. "I got your old room set up, the same way you left it. I'm not sure if we got them all, but I even had Tomas set out your dolls...the ones you used to say were your fashion models."

I nod, but my throat is tight. I don't say the words that sit at the back of my mouth.

For how long?

Lolo clears his throat. "And Tomas?"

I stare at Lolo, feeling a little taken aback. "What about him?"

My grandparents exchange a look that I don't understand.

"He's been with us almost a year now," Lolo says, leaning back in his chair. "Since around the time...well." He trails off.

Since I got sick.

Something stirs inside me, like a thread pulling tight.

Lola clears her throat. "You don't mind him knowing, do you?"

"Knowing?" I echo.

Lolo studies me. "You've always been private about certain things. We just want to make sure you're comfortable with having someone else around."

"He might find out, eventually," Lola adds cautiously.

I think of his hands gripping the motorcycle, the controlled strength in the way he moves, even in the way he touched my hair.

"He's quiet," I say, as if that answers everything, trying to ignore the heat rushing up my neck. "He seems very sincere. I don't think he'll be a problem."

"He's good," concurs Lola. "He takes care of the farm. Never asks for anything. When your Lolo found him, he was sick. Rain-drenched and hardly able to stand."

Lolo nods. "I was on my way to the chapel early that morning. The storm had passed, but the ground was still wet. I found him there, sitting by the statue of Santo Tomas, barely conscious."

The image forms in my mind, unbidden. "He never told me that."

"He wouldn't," Lola says softly. "That boy...he does not ask for pity."

"No memory. No name. Doctor Anas did everything he could with him, but got nowhere." Lolo sighs, remembering. "Your Lola and I took him in, let him rest. When he got better, he started helping out around the farm. Never once complained."

"So, Tomas isn't his real name?"

Lolo chuckles. "No. I pulled some strings at the municipality. Tomas Makalbang. Took the names from our two adjacent villages."

"You should have consulted me," I say, wrinkling my nose. "I could've come up with something cooler. Like Duncan. Or Bryce. Something very Netflix."

Lolo snorts, shaking his head. "Duncan? Bryce? Good lord, Helena."

Lola giggles, covering her mouth. "*Ay, apo.* You really have been in the city too long."

"Where does he stay?" I ask, the words slipping out before I can catch them.

Lolo gestures toward the back of the farm. "He has a small hut at the edge of the farm. Built it up himself, little by little. He's very good with these things. Good with his hands. And he's a hard worker. Knows the land better than I do now." There is no mistaking the pride in my grandfather's voice.

I look toward the darkened window.

At the edge of the farm, alone.

Lolo follows my gaze. "He's probably in there now, doing whatever it is he does. He's a bit of a loner, doesn't really want to be with people. We tried to get him to play basketball with the other boys, maybe meet girls during fiestas...but he keeps telling us he just wants to be here on his own."

Lola shrugs. "He prefers it that way, I think. But he'll be there if you need anything. We all are."

"He watches out for us, though," adds Lolo. "That's more important to me and your Lola, especially with you home."

The word settles in my chest.

Home.

"I hope...I won't be any trouble for you."

There it is.

Everything I've been meaning to say since I got here. Everything I couldn't bring myself to admit.

Until now.

I just want to be home when it happens. That's all.

Lolo stands suddenly, moving around the table, and before I can react, he pulls me into his arms.

I freeze. Then, slowly, I melt into his embrace, pressing my face into his shoulder. He smells of coffee and earth, of all the summers I spent by his side, of everything I had forgotten.

I know, in that moment, that he understands.

He knows why I am here.

He knows I have chosen this place.

Lola joins us, wrapping her arms around me from the other side, smelling of sugar and warm mornings.

"No," she says. "You're home, Helena. Don't ever say that again."

I squeeze my eyes shut, forcing back the tears, holding on to them for as long as I can.

For as long as I have left.

Something pulls me from sleep.

A flicker of light outside my window.

Fireflies.

I slip out of bed, my feet soundless against the wooden floor as I move toward the door and down the narrow staircase. The air outside is warm, carrying the scent of damp grass and mango blossoms.

The fireflies hover by the porch, glowing softly, leading me down the path toward the back of the farm.

I don't realize where I am going until I see him.

Tomas.

He is sitting on the steps of his hut, facing the open fields. Bare-chested, his skin dark against the soft glow of the moon.

I stop, suddenly unsure. I should turn back.

He doesn't look at me immediately, but I know he feels me.

"Can't sleep?" His voice is deep, steady, a low vibration that settles into my bones.

I shake my head. "No."

I step closer, and he moves to the side, making space. An invitation.

I realize, too late, that I did not put on a bra before stepping outside.

His gaze flickers, barely perceptible, down to the thin fabric of my shirt, then back to my face. He looks away.

I swallow. I should have stayed in bed.

But I didn't.

And I don't want to leave.

I sit beside him, the wooden steps warm beneath my legs. The farm stretches out before us, endless in the shadows. The air is alive with the gentle sound of crickets and the soft rustle of wind through the *santan* flowers.

For a moment, neither of us speaks.

"You grew up here," he finally says, breaking the silence. "But you left."

I nod. "My parents thought it was best."

He doesn't say anything for a long time.

"And now?"

I breathe in slowly, my gaze moving from the fields to him, seated barely a foot away. "Now, I'm here."

Something flickers across his face. Something almost like relief. Or maybe I imagined it.

We don't say anything more.

I watch the fireflies move around us, small golden lights against the dark.

Then I glance at him again.

Moonlight spills through the clouds and settles on him, turning his skin to bronze. I can see the sharp lines of his face, the steady rise and fall of his shoulders with each slow breath.

I know I shouldn't be looking.

I tell myself to stop. To look away, to breathe, to think of anything else.

But I don't.

I look. Again and again.

And he doesn't stop me.

Chapter 4

The Fields She Knew

TOMAS

She should not be here.

But she is.

The night clings to her skin, to the soft cotton of her shirt, the hem of her shorts barely brushing her thighs. The moonlight settles on her like something sacred, something meant to be worshipped.

She is not a child anymore.

I should send her back inside.

But I do not.

Instead, I let her watch me through half-lidded eyes, saying nothing as the silence stretches and simmers between us. The fireflies swirl around her as if they know her, as if they have danced for her before and still remember the shape of her.

She hesitates, just for a breath, her gaze lingering on mine with questions she is not ready to ask. Then she looks away.

The warmth of her seeps into my skin, and I grip the edge of the step to keep from reaching for her.

She looks out over the fields, eyes distant, thoughtful. "It looks smaller than I remember."

I glance at her, at the soft curve of her profile, the way the breeze moves her hair. "You were smaller then."

She laughs softly. "That's true."

Something settles between us, heavy with everything we are not saying. I should not be this close to her. But I do not move.

She turns to me, eyes curious. "It must be hard. Lolo and Lola told me how you got here."

I tense. I have spent a year keeping my past buried beneath my skin, hidden behind quiet obedience.

She is looking at me now. Really looking.

I swallow. "I had nowhere else to go. I've made my peace with it."

She studies me carefully. "You don't remember anything before that?"

I breathe out slowly, trying to find an answer she would understand.

What am I supposed to say? That I remember everything? That I have been here longer than she knows?

I shake my head. "Not much."

She nods as if accepting this answer, as if she already suspected

I was not telling the whole truth. She does not press. Instead, she leans back, her gaze drifting up toward the sky.

"I used to run through these fields at night," she says. "Before I left. I'd catch fireflies in my hands and pretend they were tiny stars."

She lifts a hand now, and one of the fireflies lands on the tip of her finger, its light pulsing gently.

Something twists in my chest. She does not know what she is to me.

I turn to her before I can stop myself. Her skin glows in the dim light. Strands of her hair flutter softly in the breeze.

I have seen her a thousand times before. But not like this.

She glances at me again, and I do not look away.

"You're beautiful," I say, the words slipping from my lips.

She stills.

I brace myself for her to recoil, to remind me of the line I am meant to never cross.

But she does not.

Instead, her gaze softens.

She touches the firefly lightly, then lets it go. "Thank you. For taking care of them."

I frown slightly. "Who?"

"My grandparents," she says. "They seem to like you a lot."

I nod. "They're very good to me."

A hint of a smile curves her lips. "They love you. I should be jealous, but I'm not. I'm glad they've got you."

I hesitate, feeling the weight of those words settle deep inside me. I do not know how to say what I feel, so I speak the only truth I know. "They are the only family I have."

She nods, understanding what is left unsaid. The same ache lingers between us. The knowing. The loss.

Dawn begins to stretch across the horizon, pale gold bleeding into the dark. The farm stirs to life before us, slowly, waking with the first breath of morning.

I stand, taking only seconds to pull on my shirt and tie my hair. "I'll walk you back."

She hesitates, then nods, rising to her feet.

We move toward the house, silent, steps measured, as if neither of us want this moment to end. I feel her beside me, feel the way she carries this place in her bones, the way it pulls her back even as she tries to hold herself together.

I clear my throat. "I'm glad you're home."

She looks up at me, something unspoken behind her eyes.

"They missed you," I say, my voice softer now. "Your grandparents."

Her lips part, but she does not speak. Her eyes shine, just barely.

Then she looks away. A breath. A nod.

We reach the door, and I turn to her.

"I'll make breakfast," I say. My voice is rough, but steady.

She nods. "I'll help."

Before I can reply, she leans up on her toes and presses a kiss to my cheek.

Soft. Barely there. But it destroys me.

She gives me one last look before slipping inside the house.

I try to catch my breath, watching the light of morning spill across the fields, chasing away the dark.

And I wonder if I will ever be able to let her go.

Chapter 5

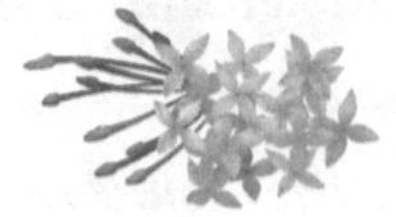

The Red Omen

HELENA

The house is already alive when I wake up.

Sunlight streams through the wooden shutters, the scent of coffee and warm rice drifting through the air. I sit up, stretching, my body still heavy with sleep.

I reach for my phone, determined not to delay the inevitable.

I dial my mother's number. The conversation is short, careful.

She asks how I'm feeling, if I've been taking my medicine. My father talks about an upcoming business trip, the quarterly reports, something about the market.

No one brings up what we're all thinking. No one says the

word *hospital* or *prognosis*. It's like we're saying the lines of a badly-written *telenovela*.

After I hang up, I call Janine.

"My queen!" she answers on the second ring, her voice bright, crackling with energy. *"Still alive?"*

"Barely," I say, half-laughing. "How's Iloilo?"

"A total disaster," Janine groans. *"I'm prepping for the new school year and dying because I have no idea what to wear for the acquaintance party without you. My entire fashion sense is in crisis."*

I laugh. "You'll survive."

"Will I?" she wails. *"I almost wore the same top to two events last week. Twice, Helena, twice! I need you back, please. Even just for outfit approval."*

"You'll be fine."

"I might cry in front of a freshman. It's going to be tragic. My reputation will be ruined."

I giggle, sinking deeper into my pillow. "Some things never change."

"Unlike you," Janine says, her voice turning softer. *"You sound...tired."*

"I am."

She pauses. *"Hel...I know we talked about this, but have you reconsidered treatment? Maybe come back to school? We could find someone better. A new specialist. Or...you know, I could come there. Just say the word. I'll keep you company. We'll binge all the shows we never finished."*

"You don't have to do that, Jan."

"Don't make me beg, babe. You know I will."

I smile. "Let's talk about something else. So...met anyone interesting during registration?"

Janine sighs. *"Nope. Zero. Zilch. All the straight guys here are either taken, toxic, or tragically boring. Same old boys with the same old haircuts and inflated egos. I'll keep focusing on the student council and my grades like before. Helps keep things straightforward."*

"Honestly, that's probably smart," I say quietly. "You're right not to rush into anything. Especially after...you know."

She doesn't hesitate. *"Yeah. After what happened with you and Adrian? I don't blame you. I hope he hasn't been bothering you anymore."*

I hesitate. "Not directly."

"Good. Because the past year has been awful trying to keep him away from you." Her voice hardens. *"The way he was looking for you, the messages, the constant calls. He's like a self-entitled rabid animal hunting his prey. He wouldn't take no for an answer."*

I press the heel of my hand against my eyes. "Thank you. For protecting me."

"Always," Janine says fiercely. *"You're my best friend. I'd hex him myself if I could. And it's not just me. Half the student council's been keeping tabs on campus visits. Adrian's been dropping by during registration and asking around. Everyone's been trying to keep him out—making excuses, rerouting him, calling security if they need to. They've been merciless, because they answer to me, of course."*

I chuckle, touched and a little overwhelmed. "Classic Janine. But thanks, to you and everyone. I mean it. You didn't have to go that far."

"Of course we did. You're not alone in this."

"Jan, how are your parents?" I ask, wanting to lighten the conversation.

She softens. *"They're good. Busy, but they miss you like crazy. Mama made* lumpia *last week and got all sentimental because you weren't there to fight me for the last piece."*

I laugh softly. "Tell them I miss them too. I miss all of you."

"They ask about you all the time," she says. *"Papa still insists no one can match your taste in picking ties. Remember the green one from, like, a year and a half ago? He got promoted because he wore it to his interview."*

"He's just saying that because I hooked him up with a designer for his suits," I tease. "And your mom just loves it."

She giggles. *"True. But also, facts. You need to come visit us in the city. Even for a weekend. I'll throw you a party."*

"Maybe," I say, though we both know it's a hard maybe.

Still, her words warm me. For a moment, it almost feels like I could go back. Like something still waits for me.

"And what about Lola Otel and Lolo Emil? How are they doing? Lola's banana fritters are hands-down legendary. Michelin-star level, I swear. Ugh, I miss those, Hel."

"I'll tell her you said that."

"Do it. She'll love it."

"They're good. Still fussing over me. Lola insists I eat more, as always. Lolo tries to pretend he's not worried, but he's been coughing lately."

"You're taking care of them too?" Her concern spills over the line. *"Saint Helena of Concepcion."*

"Hardly," I murmur, my voice dropping. "There's...someone

else helping around the farm."

Janine perks up. *"Oh? Do tell."*

"His name's Tomas."

"That's a hot name," she comments almost immediately.

"He's doesn't talk much. Keeps to himself mostly."

"Mysterious. And?"

"And...he's very kind. Lolo and Lola have pretty much adopted him."

She hums knowingly. *"Kind, hot farm boy. This is starting to sound like an afternoon* teleserye. *Come on, describe him!"*

I groan but relent. "He's tall, maybe almost six feet? Lean, but strong. Not bulky, just...powerful. His arms are ridiculous. Like, hauling-sacks-of-rice-every-morning strong. And he has these hands, big but careful."

She gasps. *"Ooooh, working hands! Keep going!"*

I laugh, heat creeping into my face. "He has long hair, tied back with this old band, and his skin is this rich shade of brown that glows. And his eyes are light brown...or maybe dark gold? I've never seen anything like his eyes before. What the hell am I even saying, Jan?"

"Shit," Janine whispers dramatically. *"I'm in love already."*

"He's got a very reserved way about him, but...he's always there. Like he sees everything."

"Hel," she says gently, teasing fading. *"Do you like him?"*

I press my lips together. "I think I do. More than I should."

"Well then. I'm definitely visiting soon. I will steal him."

I stick my tongue out at the phone. "You wouldn't survive the sun."

"I'd risk it for a hot provincial romance."

We giggle together.

"I'll visit during the semestral break, okay?" Janine's voice has become lower, more serious. *"We'll eat everything and take ugly photos. In the meantime, you get an army of hot farm boys ready to assist me when I get there."*

"Promise?"

"Promise. Love you, beautiful."

"Love you too. Don't be a stranger."

The line goes dead. And for a while, I just lie there, letting the silence fill the space she left behind.

Voices from the kitchen filter through the thin wooden door. Lola's soft murmuring, Lolo's deeper, slower cadence, a pause, then another voice.

Tomas.

I push the blanket aside and get up, padding barefoot across the wooden floor and down the narrow steps. When I step into the kitchen, I find Lola Otel standing by the table, a damp cloth in her hands, while Lolo Emil sits in his usual chair, looking more tired than he did last night.

Lola turns when she hears me. "Good morning, *apo*. Did you sleep well?"

I nod, but my gaze flickers to Lolo. "Are you okay, Lolo?"

He waves a hand dismissively. "Just a little tired. It's nothing."

Lola frowns. "He didn't sleep well, and he's been coughing since last night. I'll stay home today to take care of him."

"I can help," I offer.

Lolo shakes his head. "No, no. Your Lola needs to stay, but you can go to the elementary school for her. Sell the banana fritters. People will be expecting them, with summer classes going on."

Lola nods. "The children love them. I already packed everything."

Tomas, who has been standing quietly in the corner, is already making a move to pick up Lola's container of fritters from the kitchen table.

Lolo turns to him. "You go with Helena."

Tomas nods, no hesitation. "Of course, sir."

I sigh quietly.

Of course.

The village school is just past the rice fields, a small building with green walls and an open courtyard. When we arrive, the sound of children laughing and running fills the air.

I set up near the entrance, laying out the banana fritters on the table Lola usually uses, as Tomas points out. Of course he knows. I don't question it anymore.

Almost immediately, a group of children gathers around, wide-eyed and eager.

"Lola Otel's not here today?" a little boy asks, frowning.

"She's at home with my grandfather," I explain. "But she'll be back soon."

A little girl tugs at the hem of my blouse. "You're so pretty! Will you come again?"

I smile. "I'll try."

A few other girls giggle and reach for my hair, their small fingers twirling the *balayage* strands. "It's so soft! Like the ladies in the city."

I laugh, feeling Tomas stir beside me.

Recess passes in a blur of small hands exchanging coins and warm fritters disappearing into hungry mouths. It's easy to lose myself in the moment, in the simple joy of it. For a little while, I forget.

When the last of the fritters are sold, I clean up the table and look at Tomas. "I need to go into town to buy medicine for Lolo. The hospital didn't have it yesterday."

He nods. "I'll take you."

The *poblacion* is a little busier than the village, lined with market stalls overflowing with fruit, fish, and vegetables. Tricycles putter along the road. The smells of grilled pork and freshly baked bread mixes with the heat of the midday sun.

I walk through the pharmacy doors, Tomas following closely behind. He never lets me out of his sight.

The pharmacist checks the prescription and nods. "We have it. Just a moment."

I step back, glancing at Tomas. "You don't have to hover, you know."

He arches a brow. "Your grandfather told me to stay with you at all times."

I roll my eyes but can't fight the smile tugging at my lips. "I don't think he meant inside the pharmacy."

He shrugs. "I don't take chances."

Something warm settles in my chest. I should not like this as much as I do.

The medicine is packed up, and we walk back outside, the sun high in the sky.

"Are you hungry?" I ask, glancing at the small *carinderia* across the street.

He follows my gaze. "You want to eat here?"

I nod. "It smells good."

The open-air food stall is run by an older woman named Celia, who recognizes me instantly. "Helena, *anak*! It's been years! Look at you, all grown up."

I smile, letting her fuss over me as she brings out plates of rice, grilled fish, and salted eggs. Tomas watches silently as I catch up with her. He never interrupts.

We eat on a small table overlooking the plaza, the warm breeze carrying the aroma of grilled meat and steaming broth from Manang Celia's kitchen. I barely finish half my meal before the dizziness sets in.

The world lurches, a wave of nausea rising fast.

I grip the table, my breath shallow. "Tomas…"

Before I can say more, he is there. His hand on my arm steadies me before I can fall.

"Easy," he murmurs.

Manang Celia rushes over. "*Ay*, Helena! Are you alright?"

"I—I think I just got up too fast," I mumble, trying to regain my balance. But the nausea lingers, pressing behind my temples.

Tomas doesn't hesitate. He reaches into his pocket, pulls out a few bills, and sets them on the counter. "I'll take care of it."

Before I can argue, his arm is around me, guiding me away.

The *carinderia* fades behind us as he leads me toward the plaza, his grip firm but careful. He helps me onto a wide concrete bench under the shade of a tree, crouching in front of me, watching my face carefully.

"Better?"

I nod slowly, my breathing coming out more evenly as minutes pass. "Yeah. Just a little lightheaded."

His jaw is tight, his entire posture wound like a wire. He

doesn't like this. I can see it in the way he holds himself, too still, too controlled.

I close my eyes, the warmth of the sun settling against my skin. Just a moment to steady myself. Just a moment to breathe.

And then I feel it.

That creeping awareness, the feeling of eyes on me.

I open my eyes, my gaze settling on the *poblacion*'s main street. My heart slams against my ribs.

A red pickup truck, parked near the police station, right next to the church.

I know that truck.

A custom grille, dark-tinted windows, a scratch along the driver's side door.

Adrian's truck.

My stomach knots, nausea curling into dread.

He wasn't supposed to be here.

He can't be here.

It was his message I deleted yesterday.

Adrian, whom I broke up with almost a year ago.

Adrian, whom only Janine could keep far enough away with her network of campus kings, queens, and spies.

Adrian, who still followed me around town, who kept asking where I was. Who knew I wasn't in school, or at home in the city.

And now, he is here.

I sway where I sit, my vision swimming at the edges.

Tomas frowns. "Helena?"

But the moment is slipping. The heat, the weight, the fear...it's all too much.

The last thing I feel is Tomas' hands on my arms before the

world tips sideways, and everything goes dark.

Chapter 6

The Sea Before Us

TOMAS

She is weightless in my arms, but the weight of her, of this moment, is unbearable.

She is slipping, barely there, breath shallow, body limp against mine. I have carried bodies before. Dead weight. Blood and bone and flesh.

But this is different. This is her.

"Helena."

Her name comes out raw, almost desperate. She does not answer.

My heartbeat is in my throat, pounding, relentless. She is too still, too pale. The scent of her, fresh flowers and something faintly sweet, has become too faint.

Then she gasps. Her body jerks. Her hands clutch at my shirt, as if anchoring herself to life.

I let out a breath, trying to steady myself.

She's here. She's still here.

Her breathing remains uneven. Her dark eyes flutter open, hazy, unfocused.

And then she sees it—whatever it is.

Her body tenses, fingers digging into my chest. She is looking at something.

Her face changes. Her pulse, weak just seconds ago, starts to race.

Fear.

I know fear when I see it.

I follow her gaze, scanning the street. There is nothing but buildings, tricycles, the midday sun baking the asphalt road and the plaza concrete. Nothing that should make her tremble.

"Helena," I say, lowering my head. "What is it?"

She does not answer. She only looks at me then, as if she is waking up from a dream she does not want to be in.

"Let's go," she whispers hoarsely. "Now."

I hesitate for half a second. She's shaking now, her hands curling tighter into my shirt. She sways the moment her feet touch the ground. I catch her before she falls.

I do not ask again. I just do as she says, half-carrying her to the bike.

I grab the medicine, tie it down in the motorcycle's compartment, and help her onto the seat. She is light against me, too light, and I can feel her body shaking as I secure her arms around my waist.

The ride back is silent, a little too fast. She does not speak.

I feel every breath she takes, every slight movement of her fingers against me. Her heart is racing. Her fear is still here.

I try to speak, to ask. But I cannot find the right words. She does not want to talk about it, so I do not push.

We reach the outskirts of her grandparents' village when her hands tug lightly against me.

"Stop," she mutters against my back.

I glance at the road ahead. We are not home yet.

I slow the motorcycle to a stop. "Are you feeling sick?"

She shakes her head. She does not want to go back. Not yet.

I nod, turning the bike onto a quieter path. I take her somewhere I know. A place where the earth is still untouched, where the sky stretches endlessly.

A small rise overlooking the rice fields, where the sea is close, but not close enough to touch. Like her.

I kill the engine, but I do not move. I just wait.

She climbs off slowly, her hands clammy on my skin as she uses my forearm to balance herself. She is still unsteady, but she does not fall.

She stands there, staring at the fields, at the sun on the horizon. The wind tugs at her hair, strands of it catching the golden light. She looks as if she belongs here—part of this place, of the sky, of the air itself.

Finally, she speaks. "I used to come here all the time."

I step off the bike, moving closer, but not too close. Not yet.

"Why here?"

She breathes the air in, taking her time.

"Because this is where I was happy."

Something cracks in my chest.

I take another step toward her. "And now?"

She turns, looking at me, really looking at me. Her eyes are dark, endless. A sky without stars.

"I came back because I'm dying, Tomas."

The words drop like stones between us.

I do not move.

The world does not move.

Only her. Only her voice, soft and steady.

"Acute Myeloid Leukemia," she says, tasting the words like metal. "It's aggressive. It's fast. I was diagnosed a year ago."

A year.

She has been dying for a year.

And I never knew.

My whole body tenses at the realization.

She is still here, isn't she?

She is still breathing. But for how long?

I do not understand human illness, but I understand what it means to lose.

She presses on, because she knows I will not speak. "I stopped treatment. It wasn't working. I was in and out of hospitals, getting weaker, watching my parents pretend they weren't waiting for the inevitable."

She lets out a small, hollow laugh. "I left because I didn't want to die in that city, in that apartment, surrounded by white walls and people waiting for me to fade. I came back here because..." She gestures to the fields, the wind, the sky. "Because this is where

I was loved without expectation. Because there was magic here. I want that magic again, one last time."

I move before I can stop myself.

I close the space between us, pulling her into my arms. She is small, so small. But she is real, she is warm, she is with me.

Her breath is shaky against my chest.

"You should have told me," I say, my voice barely above a whisper.

She lifts her head slightly. "I didn't want to be treated like I was already gone."

I tighten my hold on her. "You're not gone."

Her breath catches. She tilts her head up.

And then I don't think.

I just move.

I kiss her.

It is not soft. It is not hesitant. It is urgent, aching. It is the kind of kiss that destroys and saves at the same time.

She gasps, and I drink it in, the taste of her, the warmth of her.

Her hands are in my shirt, pulling, clinging. And I let her.

The fields sway. The sky darkens. The sea waits in the distance. But none of it matters.

Only this.

Only her.

Chapter 7

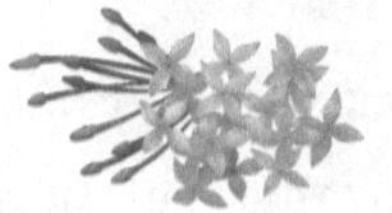

The Kiss of Life

HELENA

I have never felt more alive than I do in this moment.

The weight of Tomas presses me into the earth, grounding me, anchoring me. His body is solid, heat radiating through the thin barrier of our clothes, but it's nothing compared to the fire burning inside me.

I am not fading, not weak, not dying. I am here. I am flesh and blood and breath. And he is touching me like he knows it.

I arch beneath him, pulling him down, closer, as if the air between us is too much to bear. He is kissing me like I am something he can't lose.

I don't want to be lost. Not now. Not when his lips are trailing fire across my jaw, down my throat, his breath hot against my skin.

"Tomas..." My fingers slide into his hair, pulling gently.

His answering groan is deep, low, reverberating through me.

He is holding himself back. I can feel it.

But I don't want him to.

"Don't stop." I tilt to expose more of my neck, inviting him in.

His lips part against my pulse, his breath shaky.

He wants me. I can feel it in the way his hands tremble against my waist.

He doesn't speak, but his hands move, sliding under the hem of my blouse, fingertips ghosting over the bare skin of my stomach. I shudder, and I hear his intake of breath, as if he can feel my reaction under his skin.

His hands are careful, almost hesitant, but his mouth...his mouth is devastating. He trails lower, his lips tracing the edge of my collarbone, down to the curve of my shoulder, his tongue flicking against my skin.

My breath hitches, and my grip on his hair tightens. I am drowning in him, and I never want to come up for air.

The afternoon sun burns gold around us, but I only feel the heat of him. The heat of this.

He lifts his head, his eyes dark and searching. "Helena..."

I reach for him, fingers curling around the front of his shirt, and slowly, I pull him back down. "I'm here."

That's all it takes.

His mouth claims mine again, but this time the kiss is deeper, wilder. His hands slide up, parting my blouse between us.

He doesn't take anything off completely. He only pushes aside what is necessary, enough to touch, enough to feel.

His hands roam over my bare skin, over the curve of my waist, the swell of my breasts as he pushes my bra aside, cupping me, his thumbs brushing, teasing.

I gasp into him, and he moans like the sound itself is driving him crazy.

"You are so beautiful," he murmurs, his lips dragging over my skin, down, down. "Helena, you don't even know…"

I don't answer because I can't. His mouth is at my stomach now, pressing open-mouthed kisses, his tongue and breath sending heat pooling between my legs.

"Tomas," I whisper, my fingers threading through his hair. His breath burns against my skin, like he's burning at the way I say his name.

I should be afraid of this hunger, of the way he is unraveling me, but I'm not. I have never, ever felt more wanted.

His lips skim lower, his hands parting my thighs, lowering my jeans just enough, pushing aside thin cotton, baring me completely to him.

He breathes against me, and I shiver, anticipation making my body tense, waiting and aching.

His voice is coarse, rumbling. "Let me taste you."

My entire body goes still, then breaks the moment his lips find me.

His tongue is fire and silk, soft and deliberate.

Worshipping.

I gasp, my back arching. I feel him groan against me, as if he's drowning in this, in me.

He doesn't rush. He takes his time, learning me with his lips, his tongue, his mouth.

I can't breathe, can't think. The only thing I know is him—the heat of his breath on me, deep within me.

"Tomas," I whimper, and he grips my thighs tighter, his mouth pressing deeper, a silent answer.

I am coming undone. I feel like I am burning from the inside out.

"Look at me," he says hoarsely.

I force my heavy eyes open, and the sight of him—between my thighs, devouring me like he needs this to live—undoes me completely.

A cry rips from my throat, and he doesn't stop, doesn't slow, not until I shatter completely beneath him.

I tremble against the grass, the warmth of the sun, the heat of him.

Tomas moves back up, his lips trailing fire over my body, my stomach, my chest, my jaw, until his forehead touches mine.

"You're here," he says quietly. "With me."

I let my fingers slide over his jaw, tracing the angles of his face, the roughness of his skin. I'm shaking, but not from weakness.

From him. From this.

I press a lingering kiss against his lips.

"Yes," I answer, curling into him, my heartbeat still unsteady. "I'm here. With you."

Chapter 8

The Silent Promise

TOMAS

Wracked with the aftermath of her climax, Helena reaches for me, pulling me down to the grass with her, her body still trembling.

I collapse against her, feeling her warmth, the way her breath whispers against my skin. I have never felt this kind of release. I have never been this unmade.

Her fingers thread through my hair, guiding my mouth back to hers. The kiss is deep, hungry, pulling me into her all over again.

I brace my hands on either side of her, caging her beneath me.

She gasps into my mouth, her nails scraping down my back.

She is not done. And neither am I.

She presses against me, feeling me, knowing that my body still reacts to her, that my need for her is now even stronger, more insatiable.

Suddenly, she pushes me away, giving herself just enough room to move. She pulls her clothes back into place, smoothing the fabric, and then—she stands.

I could only blink at the sight, still dizzy from her, still undone.

And then she does the unthinkable.

She closes the distance between us, pressing her hands to my chest, and shoves me against the tree.

I barely register the rough bark at my back before she is on me, her lips claiming mine, her tongue sweeping into my mouth, stealing my breath. I groan, my hands flying to her waist, gripping, needing, binding myself to her.

She is breathless, reckless, her body molding to mine. My body reacts before my mind can catch up.

Her hands move between us, finding my belt, the button, the zipper, freeing me.

Then—*she kneels.*

She should not kneel before me. She should not look at me like this

Yet she does. I do not know how to stop the sound that escapes my throat.

She reaches for me, unhurried, as if she has all the time in the world to undo me.

"Tomas." Her mouth feels like a broken prayer against my bare skin. Her hands find my hips, slipping beneath my shirt.

I cannot breathe. I am shaking. Not with fear, but with something darker, something ancient. Something that burns and destroys, ignites and revives all at once.

She touches me, her fingers tracing the lines of my stomach, feeling the tension in my body.

"Helena," I rasp, but she does not stop. She does not hesitate.

I do not want to stop her.

The afternoon light glows around her, flickering through the trees. The wind moves through her hair, wild and soft.

She looks up at me.

I hear the soft hitch of her breath, feel the way her fingers tighten slightly around me. I do not know what she sees, only that I am lost in the way she takes all of me in with her eyes.

She leans forward, brushing her lips over the head of my arousal, so light that I almost fall apart.

I make a sound I have never made before. I do not know what it is, only that it comes from the deepest part of me.

She flicks her tongue against me, slowly. My body jerks in response. I have no control over it.

"Helena," I choke out. I am helpless, as my vision goes white.

She takes me into her mouth, inch by inch, until the heat of her surrounds me. I nearly collapse.

I have fought wars. I have killed with my bare hands. I have bled, again and again. But this...this is where I will fall.

She moves, leisurely at first, her tongue tasting, teasing, her hands gripping my hips as if to hold me in place. As if I could be held down.

I brace one hand against the tree behind me, the other tangling in her hair. I do not push. I cannot. I do not deserve this.

But she wants to give it to me.

She moans softly, and the sound vibrates through me, making my knees buckle. I have never been weaker than I am in this moment.

"You taste so good," she says.

I nearly lose myself at the sound.

I cannot think. Cannot form words. I can only feel.

The pressure coils low, tight, unbearable.

I want.

I need.

"Helena, stop," I beg, my voice breaking.

If she does not stop, I will not survive this.

She pulls away, her lips swollen, her eyes dark. "Do you want me to?"

I should say yes. I should tell her I am already too far gone.

But I cannot lie to her. Not now. Not ever.

"No."

A wicked smile curves her lips before she leans in again, taking me back into her mouth, her tongue stroking, her hands gripping me tighter. I curse, the word raw and guttural.

The world wavers and narrows down to this. To her, to the heat of her, to the pleasure that is too much, too intense, too perfect.

I cannot stop it. I do not want to.

I shudder, my entire body locking, every muscle tight.

And then I break.

It is destruction.

It is salvation.

I do not know how long I stay like this, braced against the tree, my chest heaving, my mind shattered. I have never come apart like this.

Ever.

When I finally look down, she is watching me, her lips still parted, her expression filled with something that makes my knees weak all over again.

I pull her up, wrapping my arms around her, crushing her against me. I do not know what I am feeling. I do not know what this is.

But I cannot let her go.

She kisses my throat.

I press my lips against her temple, then her cheek, then her mouth. A silent promise.

The sun is lower now. We should go.

But for just a little longer, I hold her here, beneath this tree.

In this sacred, broken moment.

Chapter 9

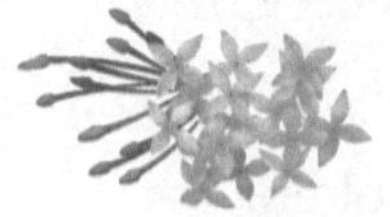

The Beautiful Burning

HELENA

I don't want to move.

Tomas is still holding me, his warmth seeping into my skin. His breath is ragged against my hair, and I don't think I've ever heard anything more beautiful.

I never thought I'd be able to feel this.

His body is still tense, as if he's waiting for something. For me to say something. But all I can do is press closer, run my fingers through his hair, kiss his jaw.

He is so beautiful.

His hair, his voice, his hands, the way he holds me like I'm something he would never let go of.

I don't want him to let go.

A breathless giggle escapes me, and his lips twitch into a crooked smile. It makes him look...deadly.

Irresistible.

"What's so funny?" His voice is low, still a little breathless.

"Nothing." I kiss his cheek, then his mouth, then nip at his bottom lip just to feel him shake a little more. His hands slide into my hair, gripping, holding me there.

"Are you sure?" he asks softly, before crushing his mouth back to mine.

I melt into him. There is no hesitation in the way he kisses me now. No holding back. Only hunger. Only worship.

His hands roam my back, over my waist, up my sides, under my blouse. Not to take, not to claim, but to feel.

"You are so beautiful," he says softly. It feels like he means all of me, like he sees beyond the surface.

My eyes flutter shut. Somehow, I know he's telling the truth. I have never been more sure of anything.

For a moment, I forget everything. That I am sick. That I saw Adrian's truck. That my life is slipping through my fingers.

For a moment, all that exists is this. Him. Us.

And then reality claws its way back in.

A lingering vision of red. A past that refuses to leave me alone.

Tomas must feel the way my body stills because his hands tighten around me. Like he knows I am slipping away into my thoughts.

His lips press against my temple, his arms pulling me impossibly close. "Helena."

I close my eyes and let out a shaky breath. I don't want to let the outside world in. Not yet.

He tilts my chin up, kissing my lips one more time. "We should go home."

Home.

The word settles into me, warm and right.

I nod slowly, unwilling to break the moment completely.

We straighten each other's clothes. His fingers brush against my skin as he fixes my blouse, his touch lingering a second too long, a second too much.

I smooth his long hair back into place, taking my time in tying it back into a loose ponytail. I love touching it. I could do this forever and never be bored.

He watches me as I do it, his eyes burning, as if no one has ever touched him like this before.

I want to keep touching him. I want more.

Instead, he lifts me onto the motorcycle, his hands strong and steady on my waist. I place my arms around him as he starts the engine. I hold onto him, a little tighter than before.

The ride to the farm is quiet, except for the roar of the engine. But the silence is not empty. It's filled with something that refuses to let go of us just yet.

I feel it in the way my fingers dig into his chest. I feel it in the way his muscles tense beneath my hands.

We are both still in the aftermath of what we have done, and neither of us wants to leave it.

When we arrive, my grandparents are waiting on the porch. The sight of them grounds me, tugs me back into reality.

Lola Otel's eyes sweep over me with the practiced ease of

someone who sees everything but doesn't always say it. "You two had lunch, right?"

Tomas nods, stepping forward to hand her the bag of medicine. "Yes, Lola, in the *poblacion*."

I force myself to find my voice. "How are you, Lolo?" I ask, turning to my grandfather.

Lola Emil smiles, waving a hand. "Much better, *apo*. Thank you for getting the medicine."

Tomas eases backward, lowering his head. "I should get back to work, sir. It will be dark soon."

Lola shakes her head, exasperated. "You never stop, *hijo*. You work all the time."

"He doesn't even take days off," chimes in Lolo, chuckling.

Their words settle somewhere deep in my chest. Of course he doesn't. Always giving, never asking.

I quickly busy myself, smoothing my hair back as if that will hide the way my face is burning. I hope they don't notice. I hope they can't see the way I'm shaking, the way my body still remembers what Tomas did to me.

"How is he?" Lolo asks, watching Tomas walk away toward the farm.

I freeze. Too many answers to that question.

"He's... fine," I manage, clearing my throat. "Very respectful. No problem, Lolo. No problem at all."

I excuse myself before they can ask anything else, rushing to my room before they can notice the grass stains on my jeans, on my blouse, on my skin. I close the door, my heart still racing.

I change quickly, the feel of Tomas lingering on my skin.

And then, out of habit, I move to the window.

There he is.

Working in the fields, shirt off, muscles flexing under the late afternoon sun. Like nothing happened. Like he didn't just take all of me with his mouth, his lips, his tongue—under a tree.

I can feel it, rising within me.

A fire burning, bright and beautiful and irresistible.

Then suddenly, he looks up.

Our eyes meet.

And I know—he feels it too.

And it is enough.

Neither of us can stop this now.

Interlude 1

THE NEVER LIFE

The first thing I feel is pain.

Not the sharp kind of battle wounds or the dull ache of exhaustion.

No. This is raw. A tearing. A collapse. My body is burning from the inside, as if my soul has been shoved into a dying vessel not meant to hold it.

The ember.

It is still alive, but...

It sears through my chest. It feels ancient and foreign, but somehow still mine.

It does not belong to this body. But it is the only thing holding me together. A stubborn flame that keeps this broken form breathing.

I gasp.

My throat is scorched. My chest constricts.

I look up, trying to blink past the haze.

The sky above is thick with storm clouds, heavy and weeping, rain falling in sheets. The ground beneath me is soaked, soft with rotting leaves and old roots.

I try to sit up and nearly scream. Every muscle protests. My stomach is in agony. My ribs grind against each other. I taste iron.

And yet...I am here.

I do not know where *here* is.

There was nothing before this. Not death. Not darkness.

Just...the pull.

Her.

A girl. A light.

A life.

I remember her as a child. Her laughter, bright and clear like the echo of sunlit rivers. Her small hands, plucking *santan* from their garden, trying to weave them into my tangled, massive hair. Her voice, singing nonsense songs as she led me deeper into the forest where no fear dared follow us.

I remember how I watched her from the trees.

How I stayed hidden.

How I never meant for her to see me.

But she did.

She always did.

And now...I can feel her slipping away.

I feel it in my blood, or what is left of it. My soul is bruised.

Torn. Not all of me crossed over. I had to make a choice.

The body I am in is weak, sick, broken. But it was the only one near the veil. The only one with a flicker of will left.

He was running. Hurt. Dying.

I saw him. I saw his memories.

Fleeting images of pain and water and rage. He had a name, but it no longer matters.

This body is not mine.

And yet it is the only way I can return to her.

The ember pulses beneath my ribs, burning a path through muscle and bone. It is trying to mend what cannot be mended. I can feel the rot burning out of me. The wounds in this human flesh are stitching themselves closed, but the cost is high.

I am growing weaker.

I push myself to my feet. My legs buckle. My skin is on fire, but I move.

I must move.

My mind pulls at threads I do not understand. I know not where I am, but the trees sway around me like old companions. I stumble down a path slick with moss and wet dirt.

Wind howls through the canopy. Rain lashes against my face.

Cold. Unrelenting. Cleansing.

I stagger forward as the downpour soaks through the fabric clinging to this stolen skin. The blood washes away. The filth, the salt, the death. All of it erased by the sky's weeping.

My vision blurs. My breath comes in ragged gasps. The ember inside me dims. Not gone, but waning.

A structure appears ahead. Wood. Stone. A strange shape planted into its peak.

I stagger toward it.

The door is open. The wind weaves its way through. I collapse just inside the threshold, dragging my weight forward until I am at the foot of a wooden figure.

It appears to be a man carved in long robes, his hand raised.

I collapse beside him. The wood is cool against my cheek.

And then—I see him.

An old man. He stops in his tracks when he sees me.

His eyes widen, and after a heartbeat, he moves toward me, steps careful but sure. He approaches with the quiet authority of someone who knows this place, who has seen miracles and madness in equal measure.

"*Hijo*, are you alright?" he asks, voice rough with age but brimming with concern. "What happened to you?"

His hand hovers at his side as if he wants to reach out, to help, but is unsure if I am real. A man speaking to a ghost. Or perhaps something worse.

I try to speak, but my throat fails me.

My body trembles. My vision begins to tunnel.

The last thing I see before darkness takes me again is the old man's face. His eyes filled not with fear, but worry. A father finding a child lost in the storm.

As my head drops against the cool ground beneath the wooden figure, I see her.

A flicker of her.

A child no more.

A woman, breathtakingly beautiful, yet fading. Her light is dim.

I came back for her.

Even if I must become something else to hold her once more.

The ember flickers once. A heartbeat. A memory.

Helena.

I breathe her name, through the ash inside me.

And I let the world burn away.

Chapter 10

The Tree Shadow

TOMAS

I do not sleep.

I never have, not in the way humans do. Not in the way she does.

I watch Helena's window from the shadows, standing under the mango tree closest to the house. The fireflies gather around me, pulsing golden in the dark. They know what I am. They have always known.

So does she.

She does not know it yet, not in the way that matters, but she has always known me.

I have been watching her since she was a child. Since the moment she first found me in the woods. She was so small, so fearless. She took my hand that night, and I have not let go since.

Even when she left. Even when the faraway city swallowed her whole and I had nothing but the memory of her laughter in the trees.

Even when I thought she had forgotten me.

But I never forgot.

I waited. I survived. I lived for her.

Now she is here.

And now she is mine.

I should not think this way. I should not want this. But today, under the tree, I tasted her, I held her, and she gave herself to me.

She kissed me as if she has always known I was waiting. She looked at me like she understood why I am really here.

I press my palm against the tree trunk, grounding myself, steadying the wild, thrashing thing in my chest.

I cannot have her. But I already do.

Suddenly, I feel it.

A breeze, too strong, too cold to be from this side of the veil.

A presence that does not belong.

The fireflies scatter.

I breathe in deeply, eyes narrowing. The scent is unmistakable. Old blood, damp stone, something from a place I have not seen in a long, long time.

I turn before the whisper of a footstep reaches my ear.

He is here.

Banuga.

The hunter. The shadow from my past.

I know. The one who was sent for me.

He steps into the clearing, a towering figure wrapped in night itself. His obsidian-dark skin gleams under the moonlight, his silver eyes sharp as cut glass. He wears the markings of our kind, inked deep into his arms, over his chest. The same markings I once bore before I lost them to this body.

He is much bigger than me now.

I do not shrink. I keep my strength. I always have.

His expression is unreadable, but I know what he has come for.

"You have been gone too long, Magal-um." His voice is quiet, but it carries through the night like a blade slicing through flesh.

He does not use my human name. He never would.

I do not answer. There is no point. We both know why he is here.

Banuga tilts his head, studying me, his eyes flicking to the window where Helena sleeps.

Something in me snaps.

Before I can stop myself, I move—fast, too fast for human eyes. I am in front of him in an instant, my fingers curling around his throat, pushing him back against the tree.

His grin is knowing, taunting. He does not fight me. He is letting me react.

He lets me seethe, lets me shake.

"You would break the veil for her?" He sounds almost amused. "For a mortal?"

I tighten my grip. "She is not just any mortal."

His expression does not change, but something glitters in his eyes. "Then you have already chosen your fate."

I know what he means. I have always known.

I release him roughly, stepping back. There is no point in pretending. I knew this moment would come.

He straightens, rolling his shoulders as if shaking off my touch. "The ember was never yours to keep, First Commander."

The ember.

The piece of old power that has kept me tethered here. The only reason I exist in this form.

The secret of the fireflies.

He watches me, waiting.

"You do not understand, do you?" he says. "What you have done?"

I grit my teeth. I do not answer. I do not want to hear this.

"The ember is bound to your heart, Magal-um. It does not just live inside you. It has become one with you. If you take it out, you will die."

The words strike like a stab to the heart. I should have known. I should have realized.

"I felt her," I whisper, more to myself than to him. "I felt her presence slipping away, after so many years of waiting for her, and I—"

"You changed," he finishes. "Not by choice, but by instinct. You took human form, all because you felt her dying."

My entire body stiffens. I do not want to hear this.

Her presence was fading...because she was dying. I only realized this today, at the same time I knew I have always loved her.

As this man.

As Magal-um.

As anyone I will become.

Banuga folds his arms. "It does not matter how or why. What matters is that you have until the new moon to decide."

The new moon.

My mind races. The veil will be weakest then. It will be the only time they can take me back.

He takes a step closer, his voice low. "You were a general once. A warrior. You deserve to make your own choice. That is why I am here."

He lifts his hand, revealing something bright and pulsing in his palm.

A boon. Small and round, it glows like a piece of solid light, humming with quiet power. A magic that will take me back, a passage between worlds that will vanish the moment the moon waxes again.

The ember must be returned at all costs.

I must face the consequences.

But we both know what I will choose.

I meet his gaze, unflinching. "I will not leave her."

Banuga sighs, shaking his head. "Then we have a problem."

"I have made my choice."

He does not speak for a long time. Then, finally, he pockets the boon. "I shall see you on the new moon, First Commander."

He vanishes into the darkness, and I am left standing there, staring at the place where he stood.

I turn back toward the house, toward her.

I will not tell her. Not yet.

But I know now.

Our time is slipping through my fingers.

And I will not waste it.

Chapter 11

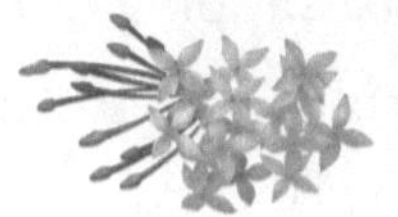

The Path of Fireflies

HELENA

I wake to light.

Not the sun, not yet, but something softer. Golden, flickering, moving.

Fireflies.

More than I have ever seen, more than I have ever thought possible.

They dance outside my window like a festival of stars, swirling in the air with a quiet, pulsing magic.

It feels like something is happening. Something beyond me. Something ancient and magical.

Then I see him.

Tomas stands below my window, bathed in their glow. Bare-chested, hair down, soft light catching on the lines of his face. He looks otherworldly. A god stepped out of the dark. A prayer answered.

My heart clenches. I know this feeling.

I push back the sheets, slipping out of bed and the house without a sound. I go to him. I do not hesitate.

The air is still cool, the blanket of night still wrapped around us.

But I know Tomas is warm. Always warm.

He watches me as I approach, his gaze steady.

I see it in his eyes, even in the shadows.

The hunger.

I close the distance between us.

"You weren't sleeping," I say.

His lips twitch into the faintest smile. "I never do."

I don't know what he means, but I don't ask. Not now. Not when I am standing before him, when I can feel his heat seeping into my own skin.

I lift a hand to his face, tracing my fingers over his jaw. His skin is taut over muscle. He looks at me like I am something to be memorized.

I tilt my face up, parting my lips. He meets me in the middle.

The kiss is slow at first. Like the dawn breaking, like the first rays of gold creeping over the fields. But it doesn't stay slow.

His hands are on me, pulling me close, fingers pressing into my back. I feel the weight of his need, the depth of it.

He pulls away just enough to murmur against my lips. "How

do you feel?"

I don't have to think. "Never better."

Something flashes through his eyes. I don't catch it, but I feel the way his body goes a little rigid.

But he kisses me again. This time, there is no restraint.

He lifts me, carries me into his little house, the wooden door barely closing behind us before his hands are under my clothes. He lays me gently on the floor and slowly strips me bare, piece by piece.

I should feel exposed. I should feel shy.

I don't.

Not when he looks at me like this.

Like I am something he has waited an eternity for.

His mouth trails over my skin, my shoulders, my collarbone, my breasts. His lips are fire, his tongue reverent, his hands mapping me like he will never touch me again after this.

I gasp when he takes my nipple into his mouth, heat surging through me. He groans, deep and rough, as if he is the one unraveling, as if my pleasure is his own.

I have never felt like this before. I have never been touched like this before.

"Tomas," I breathe, and he moves to the other breast.

He does not rush. He takes his time, learning me, undoing me, before he moves lower.

His fingers slip between my legs, stroking, testing, spreading me open for him. And then his mouth takes over.

I cry out, gripping his hair, my back arching off the floor. He groans at the sound.

His hands grip my thighs, holding me steady as he works me

apart, tongue and lips and fingers in perfect, torturous rhythm. He devours me like I am his final meal, like there is nothing else in this world but this.

I shudder, gasping, coming apart against his mouth.

He does not stop. He does not let me go.

He moves me to the tiny bed, lifting my legs over his shoulders, holding me open, helpless, as he takes me with his mouth all over again.

Then he takes me to the table.

I gasp as he lifts me onto it, spreading me open, his mouth on my breasts now, taking his time, savoring, teasing. His hands grip my hips, keeping me still.

I am shaking. I am burning.

Then he carries me again. I am leaning over the window, the cool air on my skin.

His hands spread over my hips, down my spine. Then he kneels. I feel his breath, his heat. And his mouth is on me again.

I can't stop the cry that escapes me. I don't want to.

His growl is low, wrecked. One breath away from losing all control.

I don't stop him.

He takes me apart all over again, right there, with the first light of dawn spilling around us.

By the time we are done, I can barely stand. I don't even know where I end and he begins.

In the hush that follows, he helps me into my clothes without a word, then lifts me once more, carrying me back toward the house.

We don't speak. We don't have to.

We make breakfast together, moving around the kitchen in silence, our hands brushing, our eyes meeting.

It is enough.

I am in love.

Completely.

For the first time.

And I think, he is too.

Chapter 12

The Bend Before We Break

TOMAS

I have never known love.

Not in the way of humans. Not in the way of men.

But this body tells me it is love.

And if it is, I love her.

I love her.

I love.

The morning is soft, golden. Helena is still glowing from the way I held her, the way I took her apart over and over again in the dark before dawn.

She is mine. I have never been more certain of anything.

She volunteers to sell her grandmother's banana fritters at the school. I do not let her go alone.

She smiles at me as I start the motorcycle, my hands tight on the grips. She does not know what she does to me. Or maybe she does. Maybe she is learning.

At the school, she is radiant.

Children gather around her, tugging at her blouse, playing with her hair. They tell her she looks so pretty today.

One of the teachers, a young woman, leans against the table, eyeing me. She is teasing. She is laughing.

"He's hot," she says, nudging Helena. "Where's he from? Does he have a brother or a cousin? Someone you can introduce me to?"

All the ladies giggle. Helena turns red.

I only nod politely, acknowledging them as little as possible. I do not belong to them. I belong to her.

Helena clears her throat, looking anywhere but at me. "No, no relatives. He's on his own."

She bites her lip, flustered, and I want to kiss her in front of everyone, to remind her who I am.

Instead, I let my fingers graze her back when no one is looking. A stolen touch, a claim. I let my knuckles brush her wrist as she hands over the fritters. Possession, quiet and unseen.

Her breath hitches. Her fingers twitch. She feels it. She knows.

After the school, we stop at a farm to pick up more bananas for her grandmother.

The old farmer adores her, everyone does, because how could

they not? She is beauty incarnate, soft sunlight wrapped in skin, warmth and fire and life all at once.

As we load the bananas onto the motorcycle, I pull her close. Kiss her once, twice.

She swats at me, giggling, but her body leans into mine. Her lips are red, swollen from all the stolen kisses.

I know the look in her eyes. I know what she wants.

We do not go home. We go back to the hill.

The moment we stop, I have her against the tree, my hands already sliding under her blouse, her skirt already bunched up around her waist. She is ready for me.

She gasps when I drop to my knees, lifting her leg over my shoulder. I want her like this. I need her like this.

Her head falls back against the bark, her fingers twisted in my hair as my mouth finds her heat. I devour her like a man starved.

Her cries split the silence. The sound is everything to me.

She is everything.

She trembles, her body breaking apart, and I do not let go.

She pulls me up, her hands desperate, and suddenly I am against the tree, her lips on mine, her mouth hot and wanting.

Then she kneels. She takes me into her mouth.

I nearly collapse.

I do not know how to breathe. I do not know how to survive this.

She moves like she was made for this. For me. For us.

I groan, my hand in her hair, my body shaking, and she does not stop.

We are lost. We will never be found, not like this.

We do not care.

It is not enough.

She pulls me to her, and I reach for her again, pushing under her blouse, kissing her, biting down on her breast as my hand moves between her thighs.

She gasps, and I watch her shatter under my touch.

She falls against me, sweat-drenched, half-naked, her face buried in my shoulder. She is undone, trembling.

And then, I say it.

"I love you."

She stills.

I hear her sharp intake of breath. I feel her fingers dig into my arms.

My own heart is a hammer in my chest.

But it is the truth. It is the only truth I know. I love her.

I love her.

I love.

She pulls back, her dark eyes searching mine. She is speechless. She is breathless.

I do not take it back.

Her fingers brush my lips, soft, wondering. She kisses me, long and slow.

She does not say the words. She does not have to.

I already know.

We make our way back to the farm, the weight of what we have done, what we have said and not said, settling between us.

Her arms are tight around me as we drive down the winding dirt roads. She does not let go.

Neither do I.

For now.

For as long as this lasts.

Chapter 13

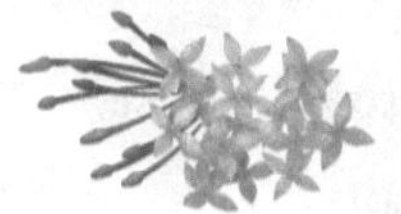

The Girl Long Gone

HELENA

I know something is wrong before I even step into the house.

Tomas and I are just coming back from the school. The sun is high, the air thick with heat, but the moment we reach the gate, I feel it.

A sudden change. A wrongness.

The front door is propped open.

My grandparents' voices carry through the air, light and welcoming. But there is something else.

Someone else. Another voice.

Measured, familiar. A perfectly calibrated baritone.

No.

I freeze. My stomach twists into a knot so tight it makes my head spin.

Tomas feels it too. I can tell by the way his grip on my waist tenses just before he lets go.

Then I see him.

Adrian.

Sitting in my grandparents' house.

He looks exactly the same.

Handsome. Lean. Immaculate.

He looks like he stepped out of a magazine spread—dark hair swept neatly to the side, his crisp white shirt unbuttoned just enough to seem effortless, though everything about him is calculated. A picture of charm, of wealth, of something untouchable.

Adrian Salvacion.

I called him my boyfriend, once upon a previous life.

The mistake I made, dressed up in designer cologne and a flawless smile.

I grip the strap of my bag so tightly my knuckles ache.

His eyes settle on me immediately, locking on like a predator scenting prey.

And then he smiles.

That smile.

"Ellie," Adrian says, getting to his feet gracefully. "Finally. I was starting to think you were avoiding me."

Ellie.

The name I wore in Iloilo City, the name that belonged to someone else. A version of me that smiled for cameras, that dressed for events, that let Adrian parade me around like something polished and perfect.

I swallow, my throat dry. I have not spoken to him in nearly a year.

But my grandparents are delighted.

"Adrian surprised us!" Lola Otel says, beaming. "He's staying in Concepcion for a while, how lovely is that? He's interning with the police station here. Imagine that! A real officer soon!"

I hear her words, but I barely register them.

Interning. Here. In this town.

Adrian watches me, waiting for a reaction. Enjoying my shock.

"Yes, I got an interesting message several days ago," he says, still smiling as he glides forward to take my hands in his.

My pulse pounds in my ears. His hands feel cold. I step back right away.

"An old group chat, maybe?" he continues, inclining his head quizzically. "A little miscommunication, I imagine. But I figured since you were here, I should come see you."

A message?

My heart drops. I remember now. The afternoon I arrived. The message I deleted. Had I sent something by accident?

I feel Tomas stiffen next to me, but he doesn't speak. He is waiting, watching.

Adrian leans against the table, casual and relaxed. Too relaxed.

"I'm happy to be here," he continues, flashing a smile at my grandparents. "It's been too long since I've been in Concepcion. I forgot how peaceful it is."

He forgot.

I forgot nothing.

I remember the way he used to watch me when he thought I wasn't looking, like I was something he could unravel if he just stared long enough. Not with affection, but with a need to know what I was thinking before I even said it.

I remember how his grip would tighten, not enough to leave a mark, but just enough to remind me he was there. That he was stronger. That he didn't like what I'd said, even if he smiled through it.

He never shouted. Never hit.

Instead, it was always the little things.

He asked questions that made me doubt myself, said hollow apologies that came only when no one else could hear them. He made me feel foolish for being upset. He would speak to me like I was always the problem. He made me think I was always the one who was never perfect enough.

And when I told him it was over, he nodded, said he understood. That he wanted what was best for me.

But the look in his eyes said something else.

He never really heard me. I know that now.

Adrian had decided the story wasn't finished yet, and he would be the one to decide when it ended.

Tomas has not moved, but his silence is loud and pulsing. I can feel him, a storm gathering over my shoulder.

Adrian notices him now. Really notices.

Then he smirks.

Oh no.

"You must be the famous Tomas," Adrian says with a nod. "With the way Lolo Emil and Lola Otel talk about you, I figured we had to meet."

"A pleasure," Tomas says, voice low and even. But there is no pleasure in it.

"Makalbang, isn't it?" The name rolls off Adrian's tongue with careful amusement. "That's the family name Lolo gave you, isn't it? How...charming."

Lolo nods. "Yes, yes, Tomas is a good man. He works hard, has the farm running like clockwork." There is pride in his voice. The same pride he has when he talks about me.

Adrian's smirk widens. "That's wonderful, Lolo. I suppose it's good to have someone strong around. This town is peaceful, yes, but accidents could happen."

I narrow my eyes, the subtle threat in his words hitting me like ice.

Tomas does not even blink.

Adrian watches him for a moment longer, then looks back at me, eyes gleaming.

"I brought gifts," he says, gesturing to the neatly arranged paper bags resting on the table. "Just a little something for you and your grandparents. And I was hoping you'd all join me for dinner at my uncle's house next week."

A trap.

I open my mouth, but my grandmother speaks first. "That's wonderful! Such a good boy, Adrian. So generous."

I feel sick. I feel trapped.

Adrian grins at me, perfectly composed.

Beside me, Tomas remains unmoving. Burning even more than before.

I have to say something. I have to breathe.

But all I can do is stare at Adrian and think—this is only the beginning.

The beginning of a nightmare.

He should not be here.

But Adrian continues to sit at my grandparents' table like he has every right to. Like he belongs. Like he has not forced himself into my life once again.

Lola sets a plate of fresh fruit in front of him, smiling warmly, while Lolo chuckles at something Adrian says. They are charmed. They don't see the noose tightening as I reluctantly take a seat next to him.

I barely hear them. My heart is thrashing wildly in my chest.

Tomas stands back, almost at the front entrance. His presence feels solid and unbreakable, a reassuring weight pressing against my skin.

Adrian stretches, rolling his shoulders with confident ease. "I'd love to stay for lunch, but I have an errand to run for my uncle." He glances at Lolo. "You know how it is, Councilor. Politics here, projects there, always keeping us on our toes. The Mayor's office never sleeps, of course."

I grit my teeth. The name-dropping is intentional.

Lolo looks pleased. "Of course, of course. Your uncle is a very busy man."

Adrian nods solemnly. "He does send his apologies for not

coming to visit you and Lola Otel. He picked out these coconuts himself, fresh from the harvest, for you and your family to enjoy." He gestures to a large bundle of plump, bright green coconuts next to the kitchen table.

"Do send him our thanks and regards," says Lolo, nodding vigorously.

"Oh, I will," Adrian says, then turns back to me. "But I'd love to stay for a few more minutes. Catch up with Ellie."

I stiffen, unable to say anything that wouldn't sound rude.

My grandfather claps his hands together. "Tomas, take care of those coconuts from the Mayor and put them in the kitchen, will you?"

I turn, about to protest, but Tomas beats me to it. His voice is polite, but I hear the edge beneath it. "Sir, do you still need me to stay and assist Helena?"

Before my grandfather can reply, Adrian laughs, light and easy. "That's really kind, Makalbang. But I'm sure my girlfriend doesn't need anyone else with me around."

I feel my entire body lock up. I want to wipe that smile off his face.

But my grandparents don't see it. They don't know.

I cannot be disrespectful. Not in front of them. Not now.

So I sit at the table, seething.

Adrian leans back, relaxed, flipping through his phone before showing my grandparents the screen.

"Ellie was the darling of Iloilo," he says, scrolling through the photos.

Pictures of me. Of us. Parties and events, shiny and artificial. Adrian beside me in bespoke suits, my smile just so, my dress immaculate, my hair perfectly curled. A life that doesn't feel like mine anymore.

"She's sorely missed since she decided to focus on her studies," Adrian continues. "The whole city asks about her. My parents miss her terribly."

I feel Tomas' absence like a missing limb. He is in the kitchen, but I know he is listening.

My grandparents smile indulgently. They see nothing wrong.

"You must bring your parents over for a visit!" Lola exclaims. "We would love to meet them."

Adrian nods. "I'll make the arrangements, Lola, once they're back from Manila. Anything for you."

I swallow my anger, my nails digging into my palms.

This is a game.

His game.

Satisfied, Adrian stands, brushing off his shirt. "I should get going. But I'll be in touch about dinner soon. And, of course, I'll be back for lunch another day."

He turns to my grandparents and bows, taking their hands and pressing them to his forehead.

Mano. The ultimate show of respect.

They beam at him.

I feel sick.

Adrian looks at me one last time, a little sneer on his face. An arrogant, dangerous curving of his lips that I wish I could rip off.

Then he leaves.

I breathe out slowly, rage burning under my skin. I push back my chair, standing, moving toward the front door—and then I see Tomas.

He is standing outside, by the gate, watching Adrian walk away.

Not speaking. Not moving.

There is something deadly in his stillness.

Adrian does not look back. But he knows.

And so does Tomas.

This is not over.

Far from it.

Chapter 14

The Tears of Ember

TOMAS

I watch Adrian Salvacion leave the Dosado house, his stride confident, as if the ground itself was made just to hold him up.

Shoulders squared, chin lifted, every step screaming that the world belongs to him.

He is tall, hair cut and styled neatly, clothes spotless and perfectly pressed. A white shirt, dark blue slacks, brown boots. He looks like a hero from one of Lola's evening drama shows. He smells fruity as he walks past.

He does not look back. Does not even look at me.

Of course he doesn't.

People like him do not need to.

They walk into rooms expecting the air to part for them, and leave convinced it will miss them when they are gone. He probably thinks his silence means power. That his absence means something.

All I see is a boy in shiny shoes and too-soft hands, walking as if he has earned a crown he never had to bleed for.

I let him keep walking.

He was never built to stay in this place.

A sleek black car is waiting, the seal stamped on the side unmistakable. It reads *Municipality of Concepcion*. His uncle's official vehicle.

A waiting driver opens the door for him. He slides inside with ease, polished and poised, looking every inch a man who owns the world. The car pulls away, leaving nothing but dust swirling in the midday heat.

I do not move from the gate.

At the corner of my eye, I see Helena standing on the porch, arms crossed over her chest. I feel her anger. It rolls off her in waves, crackling in the air between us.

But I am silent. I have to be.

Instead, I help Lolo Emil and Lola Otel open Adrian's gifts.

They react like delighted children. A bottle of fine imported whiskey, a gold-plated lighter, a carved wooden cane with an ivory handle, a red silk shawl lined with silvery thread, and a box of expensive perfumes and lotions.

Perfect for elderly men and women. Perfectly calculated.

"These are expensive," Emil marvels, turning the cane over in his hands. "That boy is very thoughtful."

I stand stiffly, my hands clenched at my sides. I can barely listen as they admire each gift, their voices warm and pleased.

Then Emil turns to Helena, his expression gentle but curious. "Why didn't you tell us about Adrian before? Such a wonderful boy."

Seated at the table like a statue, Helena has not said a word since Adrian left. Now, I see her spine go rigid.

"He's my ex-boyfriend," she says flatly. "I broke up with him almost a year ago."

Otel and Emil exchange a glance.

Emil clears his throat. "Oh? Why, *apo*?"

Helena takes a deep breath before speaking. "Because he was never right for me. He's from the city, Lolo. People like him..." She looks frustrated. "You shouldn't trust them."

Emil gives her a confused look. "What do you mean?"

"They say one thing and mean another."

Otel waves a hand, dismissing it. "Oh, *apo*, young men from the city these days are so different. Most of them aren't even respectful anymore. Adrian seems to have been raised well."

Helena scoffs, shaking her head. "He's only respectful when it suits him."

Emil frowns. "Still, it's strange you never told us about him before."

"There was nothing to tell," Helena mutters. "I never loved him."

I feel that. Like a stone dropping into deep water.

Otel sighs, patting Helena's hand. "Well, he still seems very fond of you."

I finish cleaning up the paper bags and discarded packaging, tension stretched through my limbs.

Lola has already prepared lunch.

Pork *estopado*. Helena's favorite. My favorite. The scent fills the small house, rich and sweet, the scent of sugar and bananas wafting deliciously into the air.

Helena looks at me, expectant, waiting for me to take my usual seat. But I cannot. I cannot sit here, in this house, at the table, where Adrian Salvacion's presence still lingers.

So I shake my head apologetically. "I have work to catch up on in the farm."

Helena frowns. "Tomas, you haven't eaten all day."

"I'm not hungry."

She watches me, surprised, searching my face.

"Stay," she says quietly. "Please."

My hands clench. I want to. I want to sit beside her, press my thigh against hers, remind her that I am here. That I am the one who watches over her. That I am the one who—

I cut off my train of thought.

No.

"It's fine, Miss Helena," I say stiffly. "You should have your lunch before you feel unwell again."

Something flickers in her eyes. Hurt.

I do not wish to see it.

I do not stay to see it. I turn and leave.

The second I step out of the house, I run.

Not toward the crops, not toward the small hut at the edge of the field. I run for the trees.

The moment I breach the forest line, I let the rage loose.

I roar. The sound rips from my throat, raw, furious, something between a growl and a scream. I tear through the trees, ripping branches, slamming my fists into trunks, breaking them apart like they are nothing.

I cannot breathe. I do not want to.

Adrian Salvacion.

Adrian Salvacion, on the seat at the table that should be mine.

Adrian Salvacion, calling her Ellie, as if she belongs to him. Standing there while she said nothing.

I rip another tree from the ground, the roots snapping like bones.

It is not enough.

I slam my fists into the dirt.

It will never be enough.

Then—

Pain.

A violent jolt in my chest. Something is being torn from me.

I stumble, gasping.

The ember.

It flares, blinding and excruciating. The heat sears through my veins, twisting, writhing, trying to force itself free.

No.

Not now.

Please. Not now.

I clutch my chest, pressing my palm against the fire, forcing it down, forcing it back inside.

My knees hit the ground. My breath is ragged. My vision blurs.

Then I feel it.

I touch my face. Wet.

Tears.

I am crying.

I have never cried before. Not like this.

Not like a human. Not over a girl.

Not over her.

I press my forehead into the dirt, my body trembling from the force of everything I cannot name.

I want her.

I want everything and all that is her.

But I am losing her.

Chapter 15

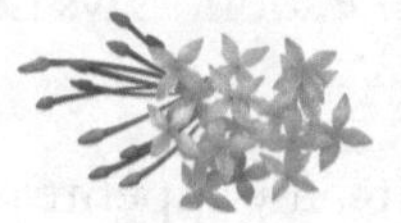

The Sorrow of Memory

HELENA

The night lengthens, stretching thin like whispered sorrow.

Tomas does not come back for dinner.

I sit at the table with my grandparents, but my mind is elsewhere. The meal of steaming white rice and beef shank soup is warm and comforting, but there is a chair left empty.

I glance at the door. At the window. Still nothing.

"Tomas works too much," I say carefully. "He didn't come in to have lunch."

Lolo Emil's brows furrow thoughtfully as he sets his spoon down. "He'll be back. He does things in his own time."

Lola Otel nods. "He does what he needs to."

I swallow. He belongs here. He is part of this house. And yet, tonight, he is missing.

Lolo leans back. "It was almost a year ago now, since I found him. I remember because there was a storm. A new moon."

Something inside me twists.

"I hope he'll come home soon," says Lola. "He hasn't eaten all day."

I look down at my plate, my appetite gone. I don't know why my chest feels so heavy.

After dinner, I insist on doing the dishes.

"The exercise is good for me," I tell my grandmother, forcing a smile.

She studies me for a moment, then nods. "Alright. Just don't push yourself too much."

Lolo and Lola retreat to their little library, the muffled sounds of the television filling the house.

I am alone now.

I wash the plates slowly, methodically. The water is warm against my fingers, but my mind drifts elsewhere.

I look out the window.

No Tomas.

I try to fight the pain churning inside me.

The past flickers in my mind. Shadows of memories half-buried, half-erased.

I remember running.

Running through the forest. Laughing.

Someone is with me. A friend.

I see flashes of brown earth under my bare feet, of green leaves brushing against my skin.

A voice, deep and warm and rumbling. Hair, long and impossibly thick, braided with flowers the color of fireflies.

Hands catching mine, pulling me forward.

And then...

Nothing.

The image vanishes.

My hands tremble. I grip the edge of the sink, squeezing my eyes shut.

No.

No. I lost those memories.

Therapy. My parents paid for it.

I was ten. They took me away.

They said I had to forget. That I had to grow up.

I force myself to breathe, counting the inhales through my nose and exhales through my mouth just like my therapist taught me.

But it doesn't work.

More memories claw their way up from the dark.

Datiles. *Falling from the trees, sweet and sticky on my fingers.*

Rain. Pouring down, soaking my hair, my dress. I am spinning, laughing.

Santan *flowers. Threading them together, weaving them into someone's hair.*

"The orange looks good with the gold," I say. "Like fireflies."

The memory rips through me like a knife.

Fireflies.

A violent sickness lurches in my stomach. I stumble back from the sink, my vision blurring.

The nausea hits fast, punishing. I barely make it to the bathroom before I fall to my knees, gagging, heaving.

My body shakes. Cold beads of sweat pop up on my skin.

I gasp for air, tears burning in my eyes.

What's happening to me?

The memories won't stop.

Fireflies.

The forest.

Gold on black.

A voice calling my name.

Heh-Leh-Nah.

I brace my hands on the floor. I try to push the memories down.

Slowly, the sickness passes. My breath steadies.

But the ache doesn't leave me.

My face is wet. I don't know if it's from the nausea or the tears.

I wipe my cheeks, my mouth.

I glance out the window again, desperation rising in my chest.

Still no Tomas.

I stumble to the front door. Step onto the porch.

His hut is dark. Empty.

The air is humid, quiet. The fireflies are gone.

Tomas is not here.

Something in me breaks.

I wrap my arms around myself, staring into the night.

I have never felt this alone. Or this afraid.

Afraid of losing something. Something I wanted. Something I never had.

A sob escapes before I can stop it. Another follows. Then

another.

I stand in the dark, on the porch of my childhood home, crying for something I can't name.

Crying for someone I can't find.

Chapter 16

The Last Honor

TOMAS

I spend the night in the forest.

The earth is cold beneath my feet, damp with the memory of rain that never reached the fields or the village. The trees whisper above me, their branches swaying like ancient hands, restless and curious.

Just like him.

I know Banuga is here.

Still watching. Waiting.

Counting the days until the veil thins and he can take me back.

I lift my head.

"Come out," I say. "Stop hiding."

Silence stretches, deep and thick.

Then he emerges from the darkness.

Banuga appears like a shadow taking form, his massive frame cutting through the night. A shadow with eyes that glint like flint.

He does not look at me like an enemy, but he does not look at me like a brother, either.

"This is a disgrace," he says, voice like thunder rolling low in the distance. "The First Commander of the High Crown. The strongest root of them all. A traitor. And worse, a fool."

The words do not wound me. They should, but they do not.

"The ember came to me by accident. From the enemy."

Banuga's gaze narrows.

"I took it from the enemy that night," I continue. "After they had captured me. I fought off a whole horde. I was stabbed seven times. I almost died. But the ember kept me alive."

I place my palm over my chest, where the fire still burns beneath my skin. A gift. A curse. A bond I never meant to forge.

"It made me cross the veil to this world. I did not steal it. I took it for the High Crown. Because it belonged to our people. Our people, Banuga."

His lips curl slightly. "And yet, here you are."

I clench my jaw. "I have spent thousands of sun-cycles protecting our kind. I would never betray them."

He inclines his head. "Perhaps. But what are you doing now?"

The answer is already in my throat. It has always been there.

"The human claimed me as hers that night. The night she took my hand, the night she looked at me without fear."

I let the words settle between us. They sound like truth. They taste like something final.

Banuga watches me, saying nothing.

"I was only ever hers," I tell him. "I never had a mate. I never looked at anyone. But all that girl ever did was touch me, and I was forever bound to her."

He breathes out, the sound rumbling through the forest.

A sound of resignation. Of understanding.

"Then let the ember go," he says. "Stay here. Stay with her. And die."

His voice is even, but there is no cruelty in it. Only truth.

"You will not survive in this world, First Commander," he continues, shaking his head. "Our kind was never meant to exist here. We cannot survive on their ignorance, their stories, their falsehoods about us. Their tales paint us as demons—monstrous, violent, uncouth. The humans fear us."

I think of Helena. I think of the way she looks at me, the way she touches me. The way she never feared me, from the very beginning.

"Perhaps that is why," I say slowly. "She had no fear of me."

Banuga looks at me as if I am already lost.

"Magal-um, I cannot undo your fate," he says, moving closer, looming over me.

The warrior. The executioner.

My brother-in-arms. My second in command. The only one who ever kept pace with me in battle.

"I can kill you and take the ember," he says. "That is my right."

The fire in my chest pulses. Daring him. Challenging him.

"But you deserve more than that," he adds, in a softer voice.

Banuga pauses. His scars gleam under the pale moonlight, cutting across his dark skin and gold markings like old wounds in bark. I remember them. I remember the night he almost died. The night I threw myself between him and the blade meant to take his life.

"You saved my life once. This is how I repay it. With honor and grace." He lowers his head. "I will see you at the new moon, First Commander."

Then he is gone.

The trees close around me once more. The wind picks up.

The fire inside me does not warm me.

I look at the sky.

The moon is partly hidden by the clouds. There are no fireflies tonight.

Only the darkness.

Only the weight of my fate.

Only loss and the inevitable.

I wait for sunrise.

And then, I walk back to the farm, disheveled, bloodied, my body aching from the wounds of the past and the wounds of my own making.

But I walk to her.

Because I still belong to her.

I will always belong to her.

Only her.

Chapter 17

The Forgotten Fruit

HELENA

I don't sleep.

The night stretches long and empty, and I don't close my eyes once.

I stand by the window, arms wrapped around myself, staring out into the dark. The air is too still, too heavy.

At dawn, a drizzle falls.

It is brief but enough to coat the world in mist and cold. Droplets cling to the leaves, the wet earth turning rich and dark. The air is crisp, cutting through the ghost of heat left from the day before.

It's colder here than in the city.

The fog is real, soft and silver, rolling over the fields like breath. Not the dark, dirty smoke of the cities my parents loved vacationing in. No concrete, no cars, no sound of a world moving too fast.

No summers were ever spent in the farm again, not since my parents took me away when I was ten.

All my summers after that were in expensive hotels and resorts, mostly abroad. Never here. Never home.

Instead, my grandparents were whisked to the city, placated with short visits, made to stay in our house like guests instead of family. I was placated too—made to forget the forest, the fireflies, the voice that rumbles through the trees.

But last month, when I made my decision, my parents had no choice.

The last wish of a dying woman.

I almost laugh.

And then I see him.

Through the oncoming sunrise, through the mist swirling over the fields, Tomas stumbles in from the forest.

A mess. A wreck.

His hands are bloody. His clothes are torn. He walks slowly, his body stiff, his head bowed like a man barely holding himself together.

What happened?

I move before I can think.

I run. Fast. Like I'm not even sick.

I run barefoot, in nothing but my thin nightdress.

I don't even feel the cold as I tear across the wet grass. My feet barely touch the earth as I sprint toward him, toward the small hut at the edge of the farm.

He doesn't see me until I'm there, standing in front of him.

"Tomas," I gasp. "Tomas, what happened?"

He stiffens. He doesn't even look at me.

I reach for him, my fingers grazing his arm. His muscles are rigid beneath my touch. His skin is cold, damp from the rain.

I try to help him, my hands pressing against his shoulder, urging him toward the hut. "Come inside. You're hurt. Let me—"

"I'm fine, Miss Helena."

Miss Helena.

I flinch at the sound of it.

The distance. The coldness.

"I just got lost in the forest," he continues, brushing past me. "I took a walk, and the rain confused me."

I stare at him. "That's bullshit."

He doesn't stop. He doesn't turn back.

"What happened?" I demand, moving in front of him, blocking his way. My voice shakes. "Talk to me, Tomas. Tell me the truth."

He only takes a deep breath, barely a sound, barely an acknowledgment.

He is ice. He is stone.

"I need to wash up," he says quietly. "And then I need to work. I should get breakfast ready for you and your grandparents."

Breakfast?

I want to scream.

My hands curl into fists, tears and frustration burning in my throat.

He moves past me again, like I am nothing.

And I can't take it.

"DATILES?" I yell.

He stops.

His back is to me, shoulders rising and falling slowly, controlled. Too controlled.

I don't know why I said it. I don't know why my chest is shaking, why my vision is blurring, why my throat is closing.

"What took you so long?" I choke out, my voice caught somewhere between wonder and pain. "I was waiting! I was waiting and waiting and..."

The world closes in.

And I am falling.

I hear my name—ripped from his throat, hoarse and panicked.

His arms catch me before I hit the ground.

Everything spins.

Then everything fades.

Before I lose myself completely, before the darkness swallows me whole...

I remember.

I used to wait for him.

In the forest.

For datiles.

Interlude 2

THE NEVER GOODBYE

I know he won't be with me forever.

But I don't know that my time with him will end so soon.

It started on that rainy night, under the bright, bright moon. Then came the days of running into the woods, knowing exactly where to find him, knowing exactly where the *datiles* would be, waiting to be picked. He was always there, in the last few hours before sunset, waiting for me.

We climbed trees, picked fruit, and splashed in the mountain streams. We raced through the underbrush, our laughter filling the air. My favorite moments were at the very end of the day, just before the sun disappeared, when I would brush and braid his hair like my grandmother did for me. I would pretend to send him home, just like she would send me off to school.

I take it back now. I hate those moments. Hate them fiercely.

Because I didn't know they were goodbyes.

I haven't seen him in almost a week.

Mama and Papa came to visit, and since that night, I haven't been allowed near the woods. They said it wasn't safe. That I might get hurt. They never explained why. But ever since, someone has always been watching me.

Sneaking out has been impossible.

Until now.

Because today, we are leaving.

My things were packed up last night. They've already been loaded into the van. Papa says I'll love the city, that I'll go to a good school and meet lots of new friends. By this time tomorrow, he promises, I'll be in a big, shiny shopping mall, doing all sorts of fun things.

They have the money now, from the handsome prince and beautiful princess in Saudi Arabia, who owned a palace like Aladdin and Jasmine.

They can give me this life now.

But I don't want that life. I want my life here.

I want my home.

I slip out before sunrise, when the house is quiet and the roosters haven't even started crowing.

There's a screw in the kitchen window grills that's kind of loose. I found it by accident one night, a few months back. If I use the tip of a fork and twist real slow, it wiggles out just enough to make space for me to squeeze through.

Then I run.

By the time I reach the clearing, I can't breathe. Our *balete* tree looms before me, unmoving. My chest heaves. I press a hand to the trunk, steadying myself.

"Hello?" I gasp. "Are you there?"

Nothing.

My heart pounds. "Please come out if you're there."

Silence.

I swallow back the lump in my throat. "I'm sorry I didn't come earlier. I wasn't allowed to. Mama and Papa got really mad when they found out I kept coming into the woods to play."

The wind stirs, ruffling my hair, but no one answers.

"Please," I whisper. "I don't want to leave without telling you."

I hate the way my voice shakes. I hate the way tears burn in my eyes. I blink hard, ignoring them.

I wait, just a little longer.

But the sun is rising, and my time is nearly up.

"Well, I guess I'd better go." I straighten my back, lift my chin. My voice wobbles, but I pretend not to notice. "I'm really going to miss you, you know. You're my best friend."

I turn, forcing my legs to move, forcing myself to believe that maybe Mama and Papa were right. Maybe I was never supposed to be here. Maybe it was always meant to end like this.

Then—

"I do not want you to go."

The voice rumbles from the earth itself, like thunder in my bones.

I whirl around, and before I can think, before I can breathe, I throw myself at him.

His arms catch me, lifting me high, and I sob against his hair—hair that smells like leaves and rain and home. I cry so hard my chest aches. I bury my face in his shoulder, shouting and cursing and getting so, so angry at my parents, at the world, at everything. His hair soaks up my tears, my snot, my heartbreak. He says nothing, only holds me tighter.

When my sobs finally quiet, he puts me down and kneels before me, just like he did the first time we met.

"How did you know I was leaving?" I sniffle, wiping my face with the back of my hand.

He looks down. *"I heard them talking. They do not want you to come here anymore."*

"I didn't do anything wrong," I say, my voice breaking. "I don't understand why I have to leave. I don't want to go to school far away."

He stays quiet, his massive shoulders rising and falling as he breathes. The golden streaks on his skin shimmer in the morning light.

I hesitate. "Can you come with me?"

His eyes lift to mine. Pools of gold under thick, dark lashes.

"No, little one." His voice is so, so sad. *"I am bound to this land. This is my home. As you are bound to your father and mother."*

I shake my head. "No. This is my home too."

"This is always your home." He holds out his hand, palm up.

I press my tiny hand into his, wrapping my fingers around his thumb.

"I'll come back," I promise. "I'll visit often."

He nods. *"I will wait here."*

The sky is bright now. Too bright. Too cruel.

"I guess I have to go." My stomach twists. "We're leaving this morning."

He lifts me again, carrying me on his shoulder. *"I will take you home, little one."*

We reach the edge of the woods, the place where the trees end and the rest of the world begins.

I cling to his neck, my fingers digging into his skin, my chest tight and painful. I squeeze my eyes shut and inhale the scent of him one last time.

Then, slowly, I let go.

He sets me down.

"Goodbye, Heh-Leh-Nah."

The world stops for a moment when I hear the words.

Because that's the first time he has ever said my name.

I want to say something back. Anything.

But I can't.

I turn and run before he can see me cry.

I don't know then that I will never come back.

That I will forget everything.

That when I see him again, years from now, I won't even recognize him.

I don't know.

All I know is that I will never, ever say goodbye.

Chapter 18

The Time Undone

TOMAS

She collapses in my arms.

Her weight is nothing, and yet it crushes me. Her body slackens against mine, her skin too cold, too pale.

Then, *blood.*

A thin, red line trickles from her nose.

A warning. A curse. A death sentence.

"Helena." My voice is raw, torn from my throat. "Helena, wake up."

She doesn't move.

A sound rips through the air.

Lola Otel's scream.

Footsteps pound against the earth, fast, frantic. They are running.

Otel is limping, half-hobbling, her hands clutching her chest. Emil is out of breath, gasping, but neither of them stop. They are old, fragile, but they run for her.

"What happened?" Lolo Emil's voice breaks. "Tomas, what happened?"

I open my mouth, but I cannot speak.

My body shakes. I do not know how to form the words.

"What happened, Tomas?" Otel shrieks, grabbing my arm. Her fingers dig into my skin.

I force the words out. "I don't know, Lola."

I look down at the girl in my arms, the girl who is my heart, my fire, my reason.

"She saw me," I say hoarsely. "And then she passed out."

Otel sobs, pressing a hand to her mouth. Her wails split the morning open.

"Call someone," she gasps at Emil. "Call Doctor Anas!"

Emil fumbles with his phone, hands shaking too much to grip it. The device slips from his fingers, hitting the ground.

I don't hesitate. I shift Helena in my arms, holding her tighter, closer.

Otel grabs at my shirt, her small, wrinkled hands clutching at me with the desperation of a mother losing her child.

"Tomas," she sobs. "She is very sick."

The words pierce through me, cutting through my panic, forcing me back into the moment.

I know.

I know.

"Lola, I know," I reply, voice cracking. "She told me. I understand."

I do not wait for more questions.

I lift her. I carry her to the house, my feet moving fast, urgent. Otel and Emil struggle to keep up, but I do not stop. I cannot stop.

My mind races.

Datiles.

Her voice, soft and bright, the child she used to be.

"I was waiting for you."

She used to sit on my shoulder, small hands clutching my hair. She wove *santan* flowers into it, laughing, saying it made me look like the fireflies.

She was never afraid of me. Even in my true form.

She used to run to me, rain soaking her through, her little fingers stuffing *datiles* into my hands, into my mouth. She never took more than she needed. She always shared.

Then the people from the city came. They took her away.

She said goodbye. She cried.

And then...

Nothing.

Night after night of empty, eternal skies.

I reach the living room and set her down on the sofa, smoothing her hair from her damp forehead. She is still breathing, but she is so still.

"Helena."

She does not stir.

The door bursts open behind me. Otel and Emil are

breathless, shaking.

I turn to them, my voice steady now. Because I have no choice but to be steady.

"I'll call the doctor," I say. "I'll take care of it."

Emil nods, too shaken to speak.

I gently take the phone from his grasp and dial the number. It rings. Once. Twice.

Doctor Anas answers. His voice is calm. Professional. Too calm.

I tell him everything.

The doctor arrives quickly. He is nearly middle-aged, with graying curls at his temples and a small leather bag in his hand. His deep voice is steady as he greets us, but he says little else. The moment he steps inside, his eyes move to Helena, quietly assessing, already at work. There is something about his presence, the calm way he moves, the way the room seems to steady itself around him.

Her grandparents are beside themselves.

Otel is crying openly. Emil is barely holding on.

"She's breathing," the doctor says, feeling her pulse. "But it's weak."

"She's so young," Otel cries. "Why is this happening?"

Doctor Anas breathes deeply before speaking. "Her symptoms are not good."

Emil rubs a hand over his face. "What can we do?"

The doctor hesitates.

"I will try everything I can," he says finally. "But I can't make any promises."

No one says a word. The weight of the truth hangs in the air like a specter of death.

Doctor Anas moves quietly, his hands already reaching into the worn leather bag. He lays out a small vial, a syringe, cotton, alcohol—everything methodical, practiced. His expression does not change much, but there is a furrow between his brows as he draws the liquid into the needle.

"This will help stabilize her for now," he says, voice low and even, like the hush before a storm. "It should help with the pain. But I will need to talk to her specialist as soon as possible."

He checks Helena's pulse again, gently pressing two fingers to her wrist. Then he leans closer, listening to her breathing, his ear near her mouth, one hand bracing her jaw. Another soft nod.

"She's strong," he murmurs, more to himself than to us. "Her body's fighting, but it will need help."

The needle finds her arm with ease. He presses the plunger slowly, carefully, then discards the syringe and wraps her arm with clean gauze.

When he is done, he stands, wipes his hands, and looks at us for the first time—not as a doctor, but as a man who has seen too many moments like this.

"Now we wait," he says. "And we pray. For rest. For strength."

His tone never rises, never falters. Something in it settles heavily. He does not promise more than he can give. But somehow...it is enough.

Otel fumbles with details, from her handbag, from a small notebook, hands shaking as she directs him to Helena's doctor in Iloilo.

"I'll get her records," Doctor Anas says. "I'll do my best, Ma'am Otel."

She nods, her fingers tangled in the blanket around Helena. She does not leave her granddaughter's side. Not for a second.

The doctor shakes hands with Emil before leaving. I follow him outside.

"You are a good man, Tomas," he says, adjusting the strap of his bag. "You take good care of them."

I say nothing.

"I have known Tatay Emil and Ma'am Otel all my life," the doctor continues. "They don't deserve this."

"No one does, Doc," I reply.

He nods solemnly. "Call me anytime. I'll be in touch as soon as I know more."

Then he drives away in his small gray car, leaving behind a home that no longer feels whole.

I stand on the porch, unmoving. The sun is up, bright and merciless. The morning mist is gone.

But I am still waiting.

Waiting for her to wake up. Waiting for her to open her eyes. Waiting for her to smile at me like she did before, when the world wasn't ending.

I close my eyes.

Datiles.

I will wait for you...and we can pick *datiles* together.

I press my fists against my eyes, swallowing the lump in my throat.

Come back to me, my love.
Please.
Come back.

Chapter 19

The Only Place

HELENA

Darkness folds around me.

I don't want to go away without telling you.

The words echo into the void, soft, distant.

A child's voice.

My voice.

I don't understand why I have to leave. I didn't do anything wrong.

The words repeat.

Over and over.

I didn't do anything wrong.

I feel it, the crushing weight of grief, the first heartbreak I ever knew.

I don't understand why I have to leave.

I feel the warmth of arms around me, the steady beat of a heart against my cheek, the sense of being treasured, of being kept safe.

But it's fading.

It always fades.

Darkness bleeds into emptiness. The warmth disappears.

I don't want to go away.

The memories unravel, twisting backward through time. Back to the forest. Back to the moment I found him.

The night was damp with rain, the air thick with the scent of earth and leaves. The trees loomed tall, whispering secrets to the wind. And there, in the center of it all, was him.

I reached out, my small fingers wrapping around a massive thumb. His skin was black with gold markings, gleaming like fireflies in the shadows. His eyes—gold, deep, ancient. His scent—earth, rain, something beautiful and true.

He was my friend. The friend I never wanted to leave.

And suddenly—

I gasp awake.

It is dark. So dark.

For a moment, I don't know where I am. The walls shift, unfamiliar, swallowing me whole. I can't breathe.

Then I feel him.

Tomas.

I blink hard, my vision adjusting slowly.

He is sitting beside me. Unmoving. Watching.

My lips part. "Tomas?"

His face remains still, but his eyes soften. He helps me sit up, carefully. His touch is steady.

"Your grandparents are asleep," he tells me. "They refused to go to bed. They waited for you to wake up, but I told them I would watch over you."

I swallow thickly. My throat is dry, my head light. "Why are you here?"

His jaw tightens, but he doesn't look away. "Where else would I be?"

I shake my head, trying to focus. "You didn't want to talk to me earlier."

Tomas does not answer. A shadow crosses his face.

"It doesn't matter now," he finally says. "You have to get better. And I'll make sure you do."

I stare at him, at the bruises, the scratches lining his hands, his arms, his face.

Memories flicker in and out. Tomas, coming in from the forest. Stumbling. Broken. A wreck of a man who had lost something he would bleed for.

"What happened?" I whisper. "You were in the forest..."

He only shakes his head. He doesn't explain.

Instead, I see it.

The way his fists clench, the way his chest rises and falls just a little too fast. He is holding something back. Something bigger than both of us.

I feel a lump rise in my throat.

"Tomas..." My voice cracks. "I'm sorry you're hurt. But, please...don't hurt me too."

His head snaps up. Pain ripples through his expression.

And then—he kneels.

His hands reach for mine, but he hesitates before touching me. Like he is afraid he might break me.

"No," he says. "Don't be sorry. I'm not hurt. I will never be hurt as long as you're here. Do you understand?"

I let out a small, broken laugh. Tears well in my eyes.

"Just get better." He grips my hands tighter. "And we'll...we'll..."

I sniffle, trying to smile through the tears. "We'll what?"

He doesn't answer. He only looks at me like I am the only thing he has ever wanted.

I shake my head. The truth presses against my ribs, sharp and unforgiving.

"Tomas," I tell him, my voice cracking, "I'm dying. There's no getting better from this."

His whole body goes still.

Without a word, he pulls me into his arms. The warmth of his body soaks into mine.

I break.

I sob into his chest.

He holds me until the darkness lifts, until the first streaks of morning light break through the window.

The moment my grandparents wake, they rush to me, fussing, crying. Their love fills the room.

"You scared us, *apo*," Lola Otel says, running her hands over my hair, my arms, like she can make sure I'm still whole. "Are you feeling better?"

I nod weakly. "I'm just tired."

Lolo Emil places a gentle hand on my back. "Come, let's get

you something to eat. You need to take your medication."

Tomas doesn't move from my side. Not even once.

I eat in slow, small bites, letting my grandparents fuss over me. The food tastes like nothing. But I swallow anyway.

The morning is soft, golden. The house smells of warm broth and freshly washed clothes. It smells like home.

A home I never wanted to leave.

"Can I go to my room?" I ask after a while. "I just...I just want to sleep."

Lola hesitates, but Lolo nods. "Of course."

Before I can move, Tomas is already lifting me. I begin to protest.

He only shakes his head. "Rest."

I let my head fall against his shoulder as he carries me upstairs. I don't fight it.

My grandparents fuss as Tomas sets me gently on the bed, tucking the blankets around me.

"I'm sorry," I tell them, my voice barely there. "I just wanted to come home."

Lola kisses my forehead. "You are home."

Tomas sits at the edge of the bed, silent.

As I drift into sleep, I feel his fingers brushing lightly against my hair.

Can you come with me? I want to ask him.

And, somehow, I already hear the answer.

This is always your home.

Chapter 20

The World of Us

TOMAS

Adrian's gifts arrive the following afternoon.

Stacked neatly inside a wooden crate, wrapped in ribbons and marked with his family's crest.

Expensive. Extravagant. Unnecessary.

Inside the crate are things meant to impress: fine woven blankets, imported chocolates, a set of luxury teas, bottles of expensive wine. For Emil, a custom-made *bolo* knife with an ivory handle, engraved with his name. For Otel, a blue silk scarf and a gold-plated brooch shaped like a rose.

All carefully curated, calculated.

A messenger from the Mayor's office delivers the gifts and Adrian's invitation, all smiles and pleasantries. The dinner is confirmed. Next week. The Mayor has arranged a private gathering, only family. The Dosados are honored guests.

Adrian, however, will not be in town until then. He has business in the city. Paperwork for his internship.

I take the crate inside without a word. Without looking at it too closely, because if I do, I might break something.

The days pass.

Helena recovers.

I do not leave the farm. I do not sleep. I do not go anywhere unless I have something to do. Her presence commands me, and I obey.

Lola Otel and Lolo Emil try to tell me to rest, to take care of myself, but I refuse. They need to take care of themselves. I will take care of Helena.

Her parents call.

I listen in, silent, bitter. They took her from here once. They cannot have her again.

Doctor Anas prescribes medication to help with her symptoms.

She stands. She walks. She grows stronger.

Her appetite returns, little by little. She begins to move more, stretch more, rediscover her body as it fights for her.

On the fourth day, she asks to walk around the farm.

I watch her. Every step. Every breath.

She picks *santan* flowers from the yard, threading them into garlands with the deft ease of someone who has done it a hundred times before.

She does not remember why she knows how.

But I do.

I say nothing. I let her weave, let her hands move as if guided by something greater than memory.

She hums softly, fingers looping flowers together, and the sound drifts toward me.

A nonsense song I have heard before. A song from the past.

Her skin has color again. Her laugh, once soft, is louder now. She is alive. She is glowing.

And I remain by her side.

Evening falls once more, cloaking the farm in a blanket of shadow and quiet.

I clean up after sending her grandparents to bed. Helena should be asleep. She needs the rest.

The house is still. The sounds I hear are of crickets chirping and the occasional rustle of the wind through the trees outside.

I have discarded my shirt, the heat of the night making it unnecessary. My body moves through the kitchen with routine familiarity, washing the last of the dishes, wiping down the counters, switching off the lights outside and inside one by one.

Then I hear it.

I hear her.

The creak of the stairs. An unsteady breath.

I turn.

She is there, at the top of the staircase, standing in the dim glow of the single bulb still lit in the kitchen. Her nightdress clings to her frame, delicate and soft, moving with her as she grips the rail. She looks unsteady, but determined.

She looks at me in surprise. She had not expected me to still be here.

"Helena," I say, moving toward her. "You should be resting."

She smiles softly. "I got hungry."

A good sign. She is stronger. She is healing.

But the steps are steep, and her body is still weak.

"Hold on," I say. "I'll help you down."

She shakes her head. "No. I'm strong enough. A few steps won't hurt."

I know what she is doing. Testing herself.

Testing me.

"Helena—"

She stumbles.

I catch her. Hands firm around her waist. Holding her steady. Keeping her close.

She gasps, her body flush against mine.

Silence wraps around us.

She lifts her head. Looks at me.

And I see it in her eyes.

Hunger. Burning and unstoppable.

Then she kisses me.

She pulls at my bare shoulders, her nails dragging lightly across my skin. I press her against the stair railing, and she moans.

Hands fumble. Reaching. Feeling. Claiming.

Her hands dig into my back. Mine sink into her hips.

She groans into my mouth, and the sound unravels me. I need her.

I need her.

I need.

I lift her, pinning her against the wood, holding her up as I claim her lips again and again.

Her hands push into my hair, tugging, demanding more.

I give it to her. Every part of me. Every aching, starving part.

Her nightdress is pushed aside.

Her breath trembles. Her skin warms under my hands.

I touch her. Softly at first. Then deeper. And more.

She shudders. Her head falls back, her hands clutch at me, her legs tighten around my waist.

My mouth finds her throat, her collarbone. I kiss. I bite. I worship.

Her nipples harden under my tongue. The heat of her becomes hotter, wetter, as my fingers slide past the thin barrier of her underwear.

She writhes.

Mine.

She reaches for me. Lower. Bolder.

Her fingers graze against the hardness straining beneath my pants, and I nearly lose myself.

"You're right," she whispers, giggling breathlessly. "I think I'm getting better."

I close my eyes. Refusing to think of tomorrow. Refusing to think of anything but this.

I kiss her again.

The night is ours. The world is ours.

For now.

Only now.

Chapter 21

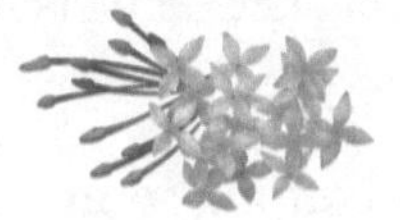

The Night of Surrender

HELENA

I don't wake up gasping anymore.

The nightmares don't chase me, don't drag me into the darkness.

Instead, my dreams begin to take shape, with soft, glowing edges that feel warm and familiar.

A past I don't fear.

A past I'm beginning to embrace.

The days pass. I walk farther, longer. I let the wind rush through my hair, let the sun kiss my skin without worrying about how fragile I once felt.

I'm stronger now. My body is mine again.

I start taking photos of the farm, of the sunsets, of the mango trees that stretch toward the sky, of the *santan* flowers that bloom in clusters of fire. They remind me of something I can't quite name, but they bring me comfort. Memories dance just outside my reach.

At dinner later that week, the conversation finally heads in the direction I dread.

The Mayor's dinner is coming soon.

Lolo Emil sets down his glass and looks at Tomas. "You should come with us."

Tomas looks up, eyes narrowing slightly. He does not like leaving the farm.

"You're family," Lolo continues. "And you should spend time with people your age."

Lola Otel nods happily. "Yes, Tomas! You always work too hard. A nice meal and a little socializing will be good for you."

Tomas doesn't speak at first. I see it in the way his fingers tighten around his spoon, in the twitch of his jaw. He doesn't want to go.

But Lolo's word is law.

"Thank you," Tomas finally says. "I would be honored."

Lola claps her hands together. "That's settled then! But, oh, Tomas, you don't have anything to wear."

I smile, leaning forward. "I'll sort it out. A trip to the *poblacion* would do me good, and besides—" I lift my chin playfully. "I've made a career out of fashion before."

Lolo looks doubtful. "Are you sure you're strong enough to go into town?"

Tomas speaks before I can. "I'll be with her."

"Besides," I add, "Doctor Anas is in town, right? I'll be fine."

It's the truth. I feel fine. Better than fine. I feel alive.

That night, I lie in bed, staring at the ceiling.

The rain begins. Soft at first, then heavier.

I think of Tomas.

I miss him.

I miss his kisses. He hasn't kissed me since that night on the stairs, hasn't touched me in the way I ache for him to.

I know why. He's afraid. Afraid I will break. Afraid he will hurt me.

But he won't. I know now.

I'm strong enough. I'm ready. And if I don't do this now—when?

Lightning flashes outside the window. There are no fireflies tonight. No moon. Only the cover of darkness and rain.

I don't hesitate.

I slip out of bed, silent as the night itself. I don't wake my grandparents.

I take an umbrella from beside the door, slide my feet into slippers, and step outside the house. The air feels cool against my skin.

I cross the farm, moving through the night like I belong to it.

The hut is ahead, dimly lit.

I know Tomas is awake. He is always awake.

I knock once, twice. No answer.

Then the door creaks open.

Tomas sits inside, shirtless, legs apart, hunched over something in his hands. A small carving. A piece of wood between his fingers, shaped into something unknown by a knife.

His hair is loose, falling over his shoulders. He looks like he is waiting for the world to move again.

"Helena?" His voice is rough, surprised.

I step inside the hut, dripping rain onto the wooden floor. His eyes take in my thin nightdress.

I swallow, my throat tight. "I don't want to go."

He stiffens.

I don't give him time to speak.

I step back, my fingers finding the hem of my dress. And I pull it over my head.

The fabric drops to the floor.

I step out of my underwear and stand before him, bare, unashamed.

The rain beats steadily against the roof. The wind howls softly through the cracks of the hut.

Tomorrow will be too late.

Tonight may be all we have.

I move forward, straddling him, pressing my body against his, offering myself to him without words. His hands come to my waist, firm and grounding.

Then Tomas moves.

Lightning flashes once more.

And he devours me whole.

Chapter 22

The Unbroken Bond

TOMAS

I do not remember what it means to be human.

Not like this. Not in the way she wants me to be.

Not even in this body.

She is warm against me, bare and soft, pressing into every aching, breaking part of me. My hands are on her skin, my fingers spreading over the curve of her hips, her back. She is so small. So delicate. So impossibly strong.

I do not know what to do. Not like this.

"I don't remember," I say, voice hoarse against the hollow of her throat. "I don't know how to do this."

I feel her pulse beneath my lips, racing, alive.

Alive for me.

She tilts her head down so our foreheads touch, our breath mingling in the thick, heavy dark.

"I do," she says. "I've done this before."

Something inside me turns cold.

Before.

Another man. Another moment.

Another memory where I did not exist.

Something bitter coils in my chest. I do not like it. I do not want to feel it. I do not want to share her, not even with the past.

Her fingers trail over my jaw, pulling me back, forcing my eyes to hers.

She is smiling, amused. She knows what I am thinking. "It wasn't love, Tomas. Not like this."

I swallow hard. "And this?"

Her fingers slip into my hair, pulling me closer. "I think...I think I love you."

Something in me snaps. A tether breaks—and a bond tightens.

She loves me. She thinks she loves me.

And I have loved only her.

I do not think anymore.

I crush her to me, into me, against me. Her thighs spread, her arms wrap around my shoulders, and I fall, I fall, I fall.

Her body is heat and fire, and I am burning, starved for the flames.

I do not remember what it means to be human, but I remember this.

I remember her.

I start with her mouth, devouring the gasping breaths that escape her lips. She tastes of honey and the night, something intoxicating, something I cannot get enough of. Her hair falls in wild waves around us, smelling of the rain, of the earth, of home. Of mine.

I kiss down her jaw, lingering at her throat, feeling the frantic thrum of her pulse beneath my tongue. She is alive. She is here. With me.

Her skin is smooth and warm beneath my lips. I map every inch of her with my mouth, from the delicate dip of her collarbone to the perfect swell of her breasts, where I lose myself completely.

She shudders beneath me as I take her nipple into my mouth, as my tongue flicks over the hardened peak, as my hands roam lower, lower, desperate to feel more. She whimpers, arching into me, offering herself without hesitation.

"Tomas," she breathes. "Please..."

Please.

I growl against her skin, trailing lower, pressing kisses down her stomach, over her navel, lower, lower. She smells like desire, like need, like something I will never get enough of.

I spread her thighs, kissing the inside of her knees, nipping with my teeth, soothing with my tongue. Her scent is stronger here, and I lose what little control I had left.

I taste her, and she cries out, her fingers tangling in my hair, tugging and guiding me closer. I eat at her like a man starved, licking, teasing, sucking, learning every sound, every plea that spills from her lips.

She comes apart beneath me, writhing, her thighs shaking. She moans my name, and it is the most beautiful sound I have ever heard.

I do not let her rest. Not yet.

I kiss my way back up, capturing her lips, letting her taste herself on my tongue. She is dizzy, lost, but she kisses me back as if she wants to drown in me.

It only takes a moment to shed the last barrier—my shorts—between us.

And then I am inside her, and she is everywhere.

She is everything.

She gasps, tightening around me, and I groan, burying my face in her neck. She is wet, welcoming, made for me.

She clings to me, trembling. "Tomas..."

I shudder, with her. "Say it again."

She does, over and over, as I move, slow at first, then deeper, harder. I take my time, stretching her, breaking her apart, building her back up again.

She whimpers, nails dragging down my back. "More."

I lose myself to the rhythm, to the sound of her, to the way she takes me, to the way she gives herself so completely. I claim her in every way that matters. We shatter together, lost in the tide of something too big to name.

But we are not done.

I do not let her go. I cannot.

She is on top of me, riding me, her hands braced against my chest, her hair cascading over her shoulders as she moves, beautiful and wild.

I lift her, spin her, press her against the wooden wall of my hut.

She gasps, legs tightening around my waist.

Again.

And again.

And again.

Her voice is hoarse from screaming my name. My muscles burn from holding her, from loving her, from making her mine in every possible way.

I do not let her rest. Not yet.

On my table, her back arched, her breasts in my mouth.

Against the window, her hands bracing against the wood, her hips lifting to meet my thrusts.

On the floor, her knees digging into my sides as she rides me once more, her lips swollen from my kisses, from my bites.

I take, and I take, and she gives, and she gives.

She reaches for me, shaking, spent. "Tomas..."

I pull her down into my arms, holding her, cradling her. I have never held anything so precious.

She presses a hand to my cheek. Her eyes are heavy, glowing with something warm and real and only ours.

I give her a lingering kiss. I want her to feel this. I want her to know.

She sighs into my mouth. "Stay with me."

"I'm not going anywhere."

Not tonight. Not ever.

As the rain keeps falling, as the night fades into dawn, I take her one last time, slow and deep and claiming.

Because she is mine.

And I have only ever been hers.

Chapter 23

The Unrelenting Dawn

HELENA

The morning after, the world feels different.

Lighter. Brighter.

I feel it in the way the sun spills through the cracks in the wooden walls, bathing the hut in gold. I feel it in the hum beneath my skin, in the slow, delicious ache between my thighs, in the warmth still clinging to my body from where he touched me, claimed me, wrecked me.

I feel it in him.

Tomas moves beside me, stirring, his breath warm against my shoulder. My entire body sings at the memory of his hands, his mouth, his body inside mine, over mine, against mine. He was everywhere. He is still everywhere.

I turn my head, watching him, feeling something deep and unshakable settle in my chest.

Love.

This is love. Real, raw, all-consuming.

His arms tighten around me, as if even in sleep, he refuses to let me go. I don't want him to. Not ever.

I should get up. I should go back to the house before my grandparents wake up. But instead, I press my bare back into his chest, delighting in his shaky intake of breath, the way his hand instinctively drifts over my stomach, fingertips grazing my ribs.

"You're awake," I say, grinning.

His lips graze the nape of my neck. "I never sleep."

I hear the smile in his voice.

I turn in his arms, pressing my hands against his bare chest. He watches me, golden eyes heavy-lidded, molten in the early morning light.

I don't want to wait anymore.

I kiss him, soft and teasing at first, but Tomas doesn't do anything so gently anymore when it comes to this.

He kisses me back, his hand sliding up my waist, pushing the blanket down, exposing me inch by inch. By the time I realize what's happening, I'm already lost.

Tomas rolls me onto my back, his body pressing into mine, the weight of him pinning me down in a way that makes me want more of him, all of him.

His golden eyes burn, smoldering, as he parts my thighs, spreading me open beneath him. He moves slowly, leisurely, as if savoring the moment, as if imprinting every inch of me into his soul.

He thrusts, slow and deep, his lips finding my neck, my shoulder, his tongue tracing a hot, wet path down to my breasts. His mouth seals around my nipple, sucking, his teeth grazing the sensitive peak before laving it with his tongue. The angle changes, and I cry out, the pleasure sparking sharp and hot through me. He feels it, senses it, and moves again—deeper, harder, filling me so completely I can do nothing but take it.

Then he guides me onto my knees, his hands on my hips, his breath hot against my ear.

"Hold onto something, my love," he whispers, and before I can reply, he thrusts into me from behind. His hands slide up my body, squeezing my breasts, rolling my nipples between his fingers, his hips rocking into me with unrelenting, claiming hunger.

I fall apart, but he doesn't stop. He pulls me against him, rolls onto his back to the floor, his hands guiding my waist as I straddle him, his molten eyes watching me, devouring me, as I take him into my body.

His hands move, trailing up my ribs, his thumbs grazing my nipples, his lips parting in a groan as I move above him. His hands tighten around me, guiding me as I ride him, the world narrowing to this moment, this fire, this love that consumes us.

When I fall over the edge again, he follows, his body trembling beneath me, his hands buried in my hair as he pulls me down, kissing me deeply, as if he'll never get enough of us.

The fire between us still smolders by the time I make it back to the house, my legs weak, my lips swollen, my body still pulsing from our night together.

I barely make it through breakfast, barely sit still while eating with my grandparents, barely keep myself from watching Tomas too much. But the tension coils tight beneath my skin, and by the time I suggest helping him with the morning chores, my heart is racing.

The kitchen is small, warm, filled with the smell of fried eggs and sweet bananas. My grandparents finish eating and retreat to the little sitting area outside on the porch, leaving me and Tomas alone.

I shouldn't do this. I should let him work. I should help, as I said I would.

But I don't.

I don't want to.

Instead, I step behind him as he washes the dishes. I touch him. Just a soft graze of my fingers along his spine.

Tomas stills, the muscles in his back taut beneath his shirt.

He stays frozen as I press my lips between his shoulder blades.

"Helena," he warns. But it's not a warning at all.

I smirk, wrapping my arms around his waist, running my hands over his stomach, venturing lower, teasing. "What?"

Tomas grips the edge of the sink. "You are playing with fire."

I press a kiss to his spine. "Then tell me to stop."

His breath shudders as my hands slip beneath his waistband, my fingers tracing his hips. He is so big, so strong, so *mine.*

I want him. Right here. Right now.

He turns, fast, pushing me against the kitchen table. My back meets the wood, and suddenly, his hands are everywhere—sneaking beneath my shirt, pushing it up, palms warm against my bare skin.

"You're insatiable," he breathes, his mouth dragging over my collarbone.

I gasp as his hands slide into my bra, his thumbs brushing over my breasts. I arch into him, shameless, needing more.

His lips find mine, hot and desperate, his tongue sliding against mine. I moan, my fingers digging into his shoulders, dragging him closer.

We don't think. We don't stop.

He lifts me onto the table, stepping between my legs. I tilt my head back as his mouth trails lower, teeth scraping, tongue soothing, lips teasing. His hands push my shorts aside, just enough, his fingers grazing the heat between my thighs.

"Tomas," I murmur. Pleading. Needing.

And he gives me what I want.

Right there in the kitchen, with sunlight spilling in, with the scent of breakfast still in the air, with the risk of my grandparents walking in at any moment—Tomas takes me apart with his mouth, with his fingers, with his body.

He is slow. He is thorough. He holds me close as I bite down on his shoulder, to keep from crying out, as my legs tighten around his waist.

Then he stiffens—and shudders. I feel him, hot and hard against me, barely restrained.

I press my lips to his ear. "You're right. I think I'm insatiable."

A groan slips from him as he shuts his eyes. "You'll be the end of me."

I smile. "I know, right?"

He growls against my skin.

And then we fall into the fire all over again.

Chapter 24

The Flicker of Flame

TOMAS

The world exists in a blur of her.

Her scent, her touch, her taste.

It should be impossible to feel this much, to want this much, to crave someone so wholly that every moment apart feels like an ache beneath the skin. But here she is, behind me on the motorcycle, arms wrapped tight around my waist, hands warm against my stomach, drawing teasing circles.

She is shameless—and I am at her mercy.

"You're greedy." I try to focus on the road ahead, on the path leading toward town.

"And you love it," she teases into my ear, her lips brushing against my skin.

I shudder as her fingers sneak beneath my shirt.

She laughs, delighted by my undoing, as if she does not already know she owns me. She presses herself tighter against my back, the heat of her sinking into my bones, curling around my resolve like smoke. I grip the handlebars harder, trying to breathe, trying to concentrate, trying not to pull over and take her right here, right now.

But then she kisses the base of my neck, and I lose.

I veer the motorcycle off the path, slowing down as we approach a bend hidden by thick trees. Helena barely has time to question me before I pull her off the bike, pressing her against the trunk of the nearest tree.

"You wore this dress for me, didn't you?" My hands are already sliding under it, desperate, burning.

She gasps, startled but laughing, her arms wrapping around my neck. "Yes, but Tomas..."

"Tell me you don't want this, then. That you don't need me." I brush my lips against her ear, my hands gripping her thighs, lifting her against me.

She moans, fingers tangling in my hair. "I can't. I'll never say that."

"Good."

And I take her.

Right there, hidden by the trees, surrounded by the gentle hum of the world, I bury myself inside her, moaning as she clenches around me, gasping as her nails rake down my back. She is heat and hunger and love, and I am lost.

We do not stop.

When I take her over the seat of the motorcycle later, when she grinds against me in a hidden alleyway near the market, when I pull her onto my lap in the shade of an empty warehouse, we do not stop.

She is my salvation.

I would die for her.

By the time we reach the *poblacion*, we are flushed, breathless, barely holding ourselves together.

Helena laughs as she straightens her dress, trying to tame her wild hair before we step into the small clothing shop at the public market.

I follow behind, watching the way she moves, the way she touches fabric, the way she eyes me when she thinks I am not looking.

She is radiant.

I should be looking for clothes, but all I can think about is how soft she feels beneath my hands, how she looks when she comes undone. My body is still aching with need, but I force myself to focus. There are only so many times I can pull her into the dressing room before she starts scolding me.

So I let her dress me. I stand still as she picks out shirts and pants, adjusting the collar, smoothing the fabric over my chest, biting her lip in concentration.

"You clean up nice," she says, batting her eyelashes and pursing her lips. "Too nice. Maybe I should have picked out something uglier so the women in town don't look at you."

I raise a brow. "Are you jealous?"

She huffs, shoving a bag into my arms. "Shut up and take your clothes."

I grin, grabbing her by the waist and kissing her senseless.

We leave town as the sun begins to set, riding toward the hill, toward our place, toward the one spot where the world feels like ours alone. The sky is burning, melting into shades of red and orange, gold and violet.

She tilts her head back, watching the colors of the sunset burn into each other. Her fingers trail up my arm, her body pressed against mine on the bike. "Let's stop here."

I pull over, and before I can say anything, she grabs my hand and pulls me down into the grass.

The world slows.

We hold each other beneath the fire of the sky, our breathing in sync, our hands twined together. I kiss her softly, gently, this time.

She pulls off her panties and climbs onto my lap, her dress pooling around her thighs, her weight settling against me as she tugs my jeans down.

She rocks against me, slowly. The dying sunlight catches the strands of her hair, painting them molten, setting her skin aglow. She is warmth, fire, the pulse of the world around me, and I am nothing but a man, desperate to worship her.

I groan, hands gripping her hips, guiding her, losing myself in the way she moves, in the way she gasps my name, in the way she presses her forehead to mine and whispers, "I love you."

My heart stops. The ember flares.

I take her again—slowly, on the grass, our bodies entwined, the last rays of the sun casting golden light over us. She sighs, moaning as I thrust into her, as my lips trace the curve of her shoulder, as my hands slide over her skin, cupping and squeezing her breasts under the soft lace of her bra.

We are about to leave, but she stops me, her fingers curling around my wrist, her eyes heavy-lidded, filled with something infinite.

"One more time," she tells me quietly.

I press her against the tree, her back to my chest, her dress pulled up and bunched around her waist.

We are both half-clothed, desperate, never sated.

I slide my hand between her thighs, circling, teasing, working her as I thrust slow and deep from behind.

Her hands dig into the trunk, her body arching against chest, and I say against her ear, "You are mine. Only mine."

She whimpers. And she comes undone.

We ride home in the darkness, bodies aching, hearts bound beyond time.

But when we reach the farm, she does not let go.

Helena slides off the motorcycle, turns to me. She does not say anything. She does not have to.

She takes my hand and leads me inside my hut, closing the door behind us.

I reach to switch on the overhead bulb but she stops me.

"I need you, Tomas," she whispers from the shadows.

I hear a rustle a fabric, a quick flash of light color as her dress pools at her feet. She presses her naked body against me.

I am undone all over again, so I give her everything.

We make love slowly—our bodies locked together, sinking into the thin mattress, into the soft heat of the night. She moves atop me, fingers tangled in my hair, her mouth tracing every inch of my skin. I hold her hips and cup her breasts, letting her take her pleasure, letting her lead me into a kind of rapture I have never known.

"You are my home, my love," I rasp against her lips. "I was lost until you found me."

Helena gasps my name as she comes once more, and I follow her, my body trembling, my heart crashing against my ribs.

I am hers. Entirely.

She collapses against me, chest rising and falling, I hold her close, afraid to let go.

But the ember inside me burns.

A warning.

When I open my eyes, a single firefly drifts in through the open window, flickering in the dark.

A message. A reminder.

This can never last.

Chapter 25

The Sweet Deception

HELENA

The morning of the dinner arrives too soon.

The weight of it presses against my chest before I even open my eyes. My phone buzzes on the nightstand, the sound rattling against my skull like an omen.

Adrian.

I stare at his name flashing on the screen, my stomach coiling. My hand hovers over the decline button, but before I can press it, the buzzing stops.

Then another buzz.

I close my eyes and exhale slowly before answering. "What is it?"

"Ellie." His voice is smooth, rich with charm that never fooled me but always worked on everyone else. "You never change, do you? Not even a hello?"

My throat tightens. "Adrian."

"There it is. Thought I was going to have to call three times in a row and get drop-zoned." He chuckles, like this is some private joke between us. "How are you, babe? It's been too long."

I ignore the nickname. "What do you want?"

"Want? I just wanted to check in. I'm back in town. My uncle and his family are looking forward to seeing you tonight." His voice is pleasant, casual, but there's something else beneath it. Something deadly.

I swallow down the unease slithering up my spine. "I know."

"Of course you do. You've always been ahead of the curve." A pause. I hear the hum of an engine in the background, the rustling of fabric. It sounds like he's in the back of a chauffeur-driven car. "Oh, and I heard Makalbang is coming too. Lolo Emil invited him along. That's...very interesting."

I don't take the bait. "Yes. Tomas is family."

Silence.

Followed by a long, deliberate sigh. "Family. Right."

The tension stretches over the line. I can hear him tapping his fingers against something—leather, maybe his watch. Then his voice lowers. "You know, Ellie, I missed you. Iloilo's not the same without you. Neither is the scene. It's been awfully quiet since you left."

"I'm sure you found a way to manage."

He laughs. "Oh, you wound me. I've managed, sure. But no

one played the part like you did."

The words strike like a slap, coated in something deceptively sweet. I grip the edge of my nightstand. "I wasn't playing."

"Of course you weren't," he soothes. "You were perfect. And I...well, I just wish you had told me the truth."

"The truth?"

"That you were leaving. That you weren't just stepping back to focus on school. That you were actually running." His voice is lighter than it should be, like a cat toying with a trapped mouse. "You made it so hard to find you."

"I wasn't hiding."

"No?" he counters. "Then why did it take me almost a year?" He pauses pointedly. "Why were Janine and everyone else so determined to keep me away from you?"

"For fuck's sake, Adrian—"

He interrupts me as if I haven't said anything. "But it's fine now. You're home, babe. Where you belong."

My nails dig into my palm. "I don't belong to anyone."

His chuckle is quiet, like he's indulging me. "We'll talk more tonight. There's so much to catch up on. I'll see you soon, Ellie."

The call disconnects before I can reply. The weight of it lingers, making my insides churn.

It's like he never left. Like we never broke up. Like he still thinks he has a right to me.

Adrian has a way of making sure he's never forgotten.

When I finally force myself out of bed, the air in the house is almost suffocating. My grandparents are cheerful, bustling about as they prepare to head to the Saturday market in town, leaving me behind with Tomas. He lingers in the kitchen, his broad back turned to me as he rinses the dishes from breakfast. He hasn't said much since last night.

Neither have I.

"Are you mad at me?" I finally ask, watching the tension in his shoulders.

He turns off the faucet, standing still for a long moment before answering. "No."

I step closer. "You've barely looked at me all morning."

Tomas grips the edge of the sink, his knuckles going white. "I'm not mad."

"Then what is it?"

He finally turns, his golden eyes burning through me. "Tell me about him."

I don't need to ask who. I could lie, say Adrian was just someone from my past, someone who doesn't matter anymore. But I owe Tomas more than that.

I swallow hard before speaking. "Adrian and I went to the same private school before college. Our families ran in the same circles. His grandfather was a national police chief. His father was a businessman in rice importation, and his other uncle was a high-ranking police official in the city. My parents adored his family, and Adrian..." I sigh. "He had this way of making people believe they belonged to him."

Tomas' jaw flexes. "You were his?"

"I was never his," I say quickly. "Not really. But he made me feel like I had no choice."

I shake my head, almost in disbelief at my own past. "I was good for his image, and he was good for mine. It wasn't love, not really. It was convenience, expectation. I thought that was enough."

His breathing changes, shallow but still controlled. "Did he hurt you?"

"I don't know." I press my fingers to my temples, trying to sift through the memories of a life that is no longer mine. "It wasn't...violent. It was a few days after I turned eighteen. He took me out for dinner and he'd rented this suite in a hotel. I just didn't feel anything. I felt empty. Afterward, I thought...maybe this is all it's supposed to be. Maybe love isn't supposed to feel like anything."

Tomas looks like he's barely holding himself together.

I let out a shaky breath, my voice dipping into something bitter. "I would probably be the perfect wife of a mayor or a police chief, all things considered. That's where it was all heading. I had a huge following in the fashion circles, sponsors, invitations to exclusive events. I wore designer clothes before they even hit the market. My face was on posters for brands that I barely cared about. I was...expected, I guess. Molded to an image of the girl everyone wanted me to be. Perfect."

"And then about a year ago, I found out I was sick. And just like that, none of it mattered anymore. I stopped going to the parties and events. I stopped posting on socials. The brands stopped calling. The invitations didn't come anymore. The perfect image I had built—gone. But I didn't care. I just wanted to live, or at least try to."

I step closer, reaching for Tomas' hand. "Then you came."

His breath catches, his grip on me tightening like he's afraid to let go. His fingers thread through my hair, holding me like I might disappear. "And what about now?"

"Now?" I wrap my fingers around his wrist, feeling the pulse hammering beneath his skin. "Now, I know it's not supposed to feel like nothing."

"What do you feel now, Helena?" he asks softly.

I close my eyes as he pulls me into his arms, letting the warmth of him settle around me. I breathe him in—earth and rain and leaves—like the forest, like home. Like the place I was always meant to belong.

"Now," I answer, "I feel everything."

Chapter 26

The Endless Fall

TOMAS

She says it, and I break.

Now, I feel everything.

The moment those words leave her lips, something raw and primal unfurls inside me.

Possession. Need. A hunger I have never known—one that demands everything.

It demands that I take her, mark her, consume her until there is no part of her left untouched by me.

I lift her into my arms, her legs wrapping around my waist as I stride across the farm, broad daylight washing over us. The morning air is crisp, birds singing their songs, but I only hear her—her breath, her soft gasps, her heartbeat pounding against mine. She clings to me, lips at my neck, her fingers clutching at my back as if she cannot bear to be apart.

By the time I reach my hut, I am shaking with restraint. I kick the door open, the scent of her flooding my senses.

Only her. Always her.

I set her down, and before she can speak, before she can breathe, I strip. My hands find her next, pulling her into me, my lips crashing into hers, swallowing the gasp that escapes her throat.

Her back slams against the wooden wall as I claim her mouth, her fingers tangling in my hair, pulling and demanding.

But I take control this time. My hands roam over her, rough and unrelenting, pressing her hips against mine so she feels exactly what she does to me.

She whimpers against my lips, and I growl in response, dragging my mouth down her throat, teeth scraping against her skin.

She's mine. Mine.

Mine.

"Do you feel this now?" I rasp against her pulse, my tongue tracing the erratic beat there.

"Yes," she answers, breathless, shaking. "Yes."

I shove her dress up, palms burning as they travel up her thighs. My hand finds her, slick and ready, and I let out a harsh breath.

"Who made you feel *this*, Helena?" I demand, pushing two fingers inside her heat.

"Only you, Tomas," she whimpers, grinding against my hand. That's all it takes.

I tear the dress from her body. She cries out as fabric rips, falling to the floor in a heap of white. My mouth crashes down her collarbone, lower, lower, over her breasts. I suck a nipple into my mouth, biting just hard enough to make her gasp, arch, beg.

Mine.

I carry her to the bed and drop her down onto the sheets, her hair spilling over my pillows like wildfire. She looks at me, dazed, lips swollen, body bared to me.

And I claim her, as I have never claimed before.

I taste every inch of her, tongue tracing down her stomach, over her hips. I spread her thighs, groaning at the sight of her, and lower my mouth.

She screams.

I do not stop.

I do not let up until she is clawing at the sheets, sobbing my name, her body writhing as I push her over the edge again and again. I savor every drop of her, every shake, every sob, until she is begging me to stop, to give her more, to take her.

I rise over her, my body covering hers, pressing her deep into the mattress. I push her arms above her head, pinning her there, and kiss her hard. She tastes like surrender.

Then I take her.

Slow. Deep.

A punishment. A vow.

A claiming, to purge all traces of the man who had made her feel nothing.

So I give her everything.

She cries out. I thrust harder, deeper, until she is breaking, falling apart, unraveling inch by inch.

"You are mine," I growl into her mouth, my body driving into hers. "Do you understand?"

She sobs, her legs tightening around me. "Yes. Only yours, Tomas."

And I lose myself.

I pound into her, over and over. I flip her onto her hands and knees, grasping her hips and thrusting until she is wailing, her fingers gripping the sheets, until I feel her come again and again.

I pull her against me, her back to my chest, my hands roaming down her bare, damp skin. My fingers find her clit, rubbing her as I thrust into her from behind, whispering her name, her real name, as I nip at her throat.

Heh-Leh-Nah.

She sobs my name, her hands covering mine, her body tightening around me. I bite her shoulder, lick the sweat from her skin, drive her to the edge once more.

And then I move her atop me, make her ride me.

She braces herself against my chest, her hair falling over her face, her breasts bouncing with every thrust. She moans, breathless and wanton, as she grinds above me, her hands sliding up my arms.

I grip her hips, slamming her down onto me harder, faster, watching her fall apart as the stars fall from the sky.

"Say it," I demand. "Say it again."

"I'm yours," she gasps. "Yours, Tomas."

I thrust up into her, hard, brutal, my grip turning bruising as I drag her to the edge—and beyond.

She shatters around me, her body convulsing, her breath breaking. And I follow, spilling into her. We collapse together, tangled in sheets, in heat, in sweat, in love.

She strokes my hair, pressing soft kisses over my jaw.

"We were always meant for each other," she whispers breathlessly against my cheek. "I won't ever let you go."

I hold her tighter, burying my face into her neck, inhaling the scent of her—wildflowers, passion, the lingering sweetness of herself.

But I do not tell her the truth.

The new moon is coming.

And I will lose her.

She sighs, pressing closer, her leg sliding between my thighs.

"You know, I'd love to weave *santan* into your hair," she says. "Like I used to when I was little. You never stopped me, not once."

Her fingers trace lazy patterns over my skin, her voice wistful. "I'd love to run with you again. Barefoot, through the trees. I'd love to find *datiles* with you."

Her words cut through me. Clear. Certain.

She remembers.

"I'd love to...stay with you forever." Her voice is dreamlike, as if she is slipping between time and memory. "I have always loved you. In every way, I loved you."

She pauses, then she murmurs against my lips, "I love you, Magal-um."

The breath leaves my lungs. My heart, if I still have one, stops beating.

The name—*my name*—falls from her lips so effortlessly, so

naturally, as if she has been calling me this all her life.

Because she has, even if she barely remembers doing so.

I watch her fall asleep, knowing I must take this moment and treasure it.

Because this might not happen again.

This might be the first and the last.

When the new moon comes, it will destroy me.

One way or the other.

Chapter 27

The Love We Claim

HELENA

I dream of him.

But this is no ordinary dream.

Now, I feel everything.

His warmth surrounds me, and I am not in my bed.

I am somewhere else, *somewhen* else. The world is golden, the air thick with the scent of rain and wildflowers, of earth and deep, ancient wood. I am bathed in moonlight, and I am not alone.

His hands are on me. Big. Strong. Not human.

I shiver as he touches me, my body arching for more, and I

know—I know this place. The trees are alive, towering shadows whispering in a language I have long forgotten, and he is here. His breath caresses my throat, his voice—low, primal, deep enough to shake the earth—murmurs against my skin.

"You are mine, little one."

And I am.

He moves over me, fur and fire and golden eyes, his weight pressing me into the soft, dewy grass. My fingers thread into his long, unbound hair, and I see him. Not Tomas. Not the man I have kissed under the sun and stars.

Magal-um.

Dark skin etched with gold. Markings of his kind. Wild hair thick and untamed. Eyes burning brighter than the fireflies that used to dance around us. The boy who carried me through the trees when I was small, who shielded me from the rain, who let me braid flowers into his hair. The creature who once held me like I was the most precious thing in existence.

I remember.

My breath hitches as he worships me.

I feel him everywhere. His mouth tracing every inch of me. His hands pressing, kneading, stroking.

Claiming.

His tongue on me follows the shapes of his fire-lit markings. As I burn beneath his touch, they glow beneath his skin, thrumming with life. Thrumming with me.

He lifts me onto his lap, my legs wrapping around his waist. I gasp, my arms curling around his shoulders. The way he touches me is not of this world.

Tender.

Deep.

Endless.

"You were always mine, Heh-Leh-Nah," he growls into my ear, dragging his teeth over my pulse.

Then he moves.

My vision blurs as a cry tears from my throat, my nails dragging down his back. His body surges into mine, and I feel myself come apart, burning alive in his arms. I have never felt like this.

Not even with Tomas.

No.

Because Tomas and Magal-um were always one.

The pleasure is unlike anything I have ever known. It is ancient. Boundless.

My head tips back, my body arching into him, and he devours all of me.

The dream spins, twisting, shifting, and I am everywhere at once.

I am seven years old, laughing as he lifts me onto his shoulders, running through the trees.

I am ten, sobbing into his hair, begging him to come with me.

I am twenty, beneath him, crying out his name as he takes me over and over and over.

I climax again and again, lost in the storm of our past and present colliding. My body is weightless, timeless.

Eternal, like the skies.

And then—

I wake up.

Sunlight filters through my curtains. My heart thunders in my chest as I sit up, drenched in sweat, aching. My body still pulses with the echoes of my dream, my thighs trembling as if I had truly lived it.

The sheets are clean. My clothes are on me.

Tomas.

He must have carried me back. Dressed me.

I clutch the blanket to my chest, shaking.

A knock at the door startles me.

My grandmother's voice is light. "Helena, lunch is ready. You had a good nap?"

A nap. That's what Tomas told them. My stomach tightens.

I swallow hard, dragging myself out of bed. My legs are weak, my body too aware of the fire still coursing through me. I grip the dresser for support, taking deep breaths to steady myself.

I have to act normal.

But how can I, when my soul is still tangled in another world?

At the table, Lolo Emil tells us they met the Mayor's Chief of Staff at the market. Apparently, the Mayor had arranged for a car to pick us up for tonight's dinner.

Adrian wants the whole town to know he has invited us.

Lola Otel, oblivious, smiles broadly. "Well, isn't that nice? I suppose it's a formal affair then. We should look our best."

"It's deliberate," I say, my voice calm despite the heavy tension in my stomach. "So people will talk. So they'll know this is happening."

Lolo nods, rubbing his chin. "The Salvacions have always been strategic. Everything they do, they do for a reason."

I barely hear my grandmother's chatter, barely register the scent of crispy *lechon*.

Then—

Tomas and I reach for the same piece of *lechon* skin.

Electricity.

His fingers brush against mine, rough and warm. I freeze.

We could have made love on this table.

Tomas only smiles, unbothered, and takes a bite, his golden eyes meeting mine across the table.

After lunch, we take the motorcycle to collect Lola's bananas, but before heading back to the farm, we stop at the hill.

It happens before I can think.

Tomas is behind me, his arms tight around my waist, and I can feel everything. The heat of him, the strength, the power beneath his skin.

He doesn't say anything.

He takes my hand. Pulls me to him.

And I fall.

His mouth claims mine, slowly at first, then with more urgency.

But this time, I know.

This time, when I touch him, when I press against him, I see *him.*

Not just Tomas.

Magal-um.

His hands roam, unhurried but hungry. His fingers slip under my blouse, brushing over my stomach, trailing higher. He doesn't stop.

His lips burn a path down my throat, over my collarbone, until he is on his knees before me.

He lowers my jeans. His mouth is there.

I break apart. Again, again, and again.

Tomas doesn't stop. Doesn't let me go.

And when I reach for him, desperate with need—

He laughs. Low, knowing, rumbling. A sound that unravels me further.

He presses me down into the grass, and he gives me everything. His weight, his heat, his strength, his love.

His hands cradle my face, his lips branding me, his body claiming mine. His fingers thread into my hair, tilting my head back, making me meet his gaze. Those golden eyes...burning, ancient, *mine.*

His voice is hoarse, somehow deeper than before. "You have always belonged to me, Helena."

I sob, my body arching to meet his, my fingers digging into his back, my world coming apart and rising around him.

I know I will never be the same again.

I will never want to be.

Chapter 28

The Power Play

TOMAS

The air inside the Salvacion estate is thick—with power, with expectation, with something sharp enough to cut.

The black SUV carrying the Dosados pulls through the heavy iron gates, rolling past well-manicured lawns, a sprawling garden, and a massive two-story ancestral house built to intimidate. I follow behind on the motorcycle, feeling every set of watchful eyes on me as I slow to a stop near the circular driveway.

A group of household staff waits at the entrance, dressed in crisp white uniforms, their hands neatly folded in front of them.

At the center of the grand archway stands Adrian Salvacion.

He looks every bit the man who was born into wealth, polished and confident, standing with the ease of someone who believes the world will always bow to him. He is freshly shaven, his black button-down perfectly fitted, his dark slacks pristine.

His eyes find Helena first, softening as they settle on her. Then his lips curl into a slow smile.

"Ellie."

Helena stiffens beside her grandmother. The name makes her smaller. As if he is pressing her back into a shape he prefers, one that fits his world.

She does not respond, but Adrian is already moving forward, placing both hands on her arms, drawing her close.

"Don't look at me like that," he tells Helena teasingly. "I almost thought you had forgotten about me, after everything we've been through together."

I grip the handlebars tighter. The urge to rip his hands off her is immediate, brutal.

Lola Otel, ever warm, beams at Adrian. "Oh, you mustn't think that! Our Helena has been getting plenty of rest at the farm, and she's been in good hands."

I see it then. The flicker in Adrian's eyes. He knows exactly whose hands she has been in. And he does not like it.

Adrian releases her slowly, but not without dragging his fingers down her arms before stepping back.

"This way," he says, still smiling, gesturing grandly toward the open doors. "My family is eager to meet you all."

I park the bike as directed by one of the estate staff. I follow the Dosados at the rear, my body tense as we enter.

The house is opulent, with shell-framed windows and arched doorways made of carved wood. Every tile gleams, every antique piece is placed just so, untouched by time or warmth.

The sight of it all is too perfect. Too quiet and cold. A place seemingly built to remember a family that no longer speaks to each other.

Inside, the Salvacions are waiting.

The introductions are polite and short, if not outright rehearsed.

At the long mahogany dining table sits Mayor Antonio Salvacion, a broad-shouldered man in his fifties, clad in a dark grey suit and white shirt, with calculating eyes and the measured silence of someone who speaks only when necessary. Beside him, his wife, Beatriz, dressed in pale pink silk and pearls, appears poised and brimming with quiet judgment.

To their left is Carmina, their daughter, statuesque and impeccably dressed in light green, her gaze lingering on me with curious coolness. She offers me an assessing glance as we are introduced, before she returns her attention to Helena. Next to her is Ramiro, her younger brother. He has the same self-satisfied air as Adrian, a lean frame clothed in a green shirt and gray trousers, and the demeanor of a young man who has never been told 'no.'

At the head of the table, the Mayor gestures for us to sit.

"Welcome," he says, his deep voice commanding without the need to be raised. "We've been looking forward to this."

I take my seat, aware of the intentional arrangement—Helena seated beside Adrian. Me, placed next to Carmina.

Lola Otel's homemade banana fritters are placed on the table.

Beatriz takes one, delicately biting into it. She smiles. "Otel, dear, these are divine. Have you ever considered expanding? Perhaps a stall in the public market? I would love to be your first investor."

Otel brightens. "Oh, that would be lovely!"

The conversation drifts, eventually turning to the upcoming election season. They speak of Lolo Emil's standing in the village and the mayoralty and councilor races in town.

Then, inevitably, the discussion turns to Helena.

"Ellie was quite the star back in the city, you know," says Adrian, a lazy smile on his face as he looks around the table.

Helena tenses. "Adrian..."

"She was everywhere," he continues smoothly, as if she had not spoken. "Fashion contracts, shows, product endorsements, feature spreads. My mother adored her, didn't she, Tita Beatriz?"

Beatriz smiles, sipping her wine. "She certainly did. Always talking about Ellie's potential."

Helena fidgets uncomfortably in response.

I can feel her discomfort. I know this is deliberate, as with everything Adrian Salvacion does.

He wants all of us to see the life she had with him. The life he believes he is reclaiming.

Then he turns to me.

"So, Makalbang," he says, lifting his wine glass. "Tell me, what are your plans for the future?"

I meet his gaze. "What do you mean?"

Adrian gestures around the room. "This life—you must find it interesting. But what comes next for you?"

The weight of what he says falls heavily into me. The words are not innocent. They are a reminder.

That I do not belong here. That I am nothing next to them. That I am a man they do not understand and will never accept.

I see Helena stiffen. Next to me, I feel Carmina sit straighter, her gaze darting around the table expectantly.

Adrian swirls his wine. "You must feel lucky."

I straighten. "Why is that?"

He smirks at me over the rim of his glass. "Because not many people get to sit where you're sitting."

Sensing the sudden uneasiness in the air, Emil speaks up. "Tomas has been a great help to us. We're very lucky to have him."

Helena's voice cuts through the tension. "Adrian, don't."

He only chuckles, tilting his head as he regards me. He knows exactly what he is doing.

"You're very polite, aren't you, Makalbang?" he says, voice light but edged. "But I do wonder. What kind of future do you see for yourself?"

Everything around us stills.

I do not look away from him. The rage inside me simmers, low and dangerous.

Helena looks at me from across the table, a grounding gaze that says everything without a word.

Adrian leans back in his seat, watching me, waiting for me to take the bait.

I glance at Helena, at Emil and Otel.

Then I turn back to him.

This is the reckoning.

Chapter 29

The Quiet Reckoning

HELENA

Silence.

A weighted, unbearable silence.

Every eye at the table is on Tomas, waiting for his answer, waiting for him to crumble beneath Adrian's veiled insult, waiting for him to acknowledge that he is nothing to them.

A man with no power, no money, no standing.

A man unlike them.

The quiet stretches, crackling like the tense air before a storm.

But Tomas doesn't waver.

He doesn't react beyond the way his shoulders tense beneath

his white shirt. He sits still, like an immovable force, his expression unreadable. But I feel it—the rage simmering beneath his skin, coiling, rising.

Then he exhales slowly.

When Tomas finally speaks, his voice is calm and controlled, so polite it's almost terrifying.

"Thank you for your hospitality, Mayor Salvacion," he says, turning to the older man with a nod.

"Ma'am." Tomas acknowledges Beatriz next, just as poised, just as formal as she is.

He moves like a soldier dismissing himself from a court he never belonged to.

Then he faces my grandparents. "I'm sorry, Lolo, Lola. Please excuse me."

Without another word to anyone else, he stands, his chair scraping against the polished floor, and walks away.

Out.

Adrian watches him go, his smirk faltering ever so slightly, but he recovers, swirling his wine glass as if this is all part of his game.

I stare after Tomas, my heart pounding, my blood boiling.

This dinner—this whole farce—is exactly what I expected. The moment Adrian invited us here, I knew what he was doing. Parading his family, his wealth, his privilege. Setting the stage to remind me, to remind Tomas, that I belonged here, and Tomas never would.

I knew. But I still let it happen.

And now Tomas is gone.

"Well," says Adrian smugly, almost triumphantly. "That was very interesting."

Something inside me snaps.

I push back my chair, the legs screeching against the floor as I stand so suddenly that I nearly knock my glass over.

"You know what, Adrian?" My voice shakes—not with fear, but with fury. "You want to talk about futures? Fine. Let's talk about mine. The one that doesn't exist anymore."

The room goes deathly silent.

Adrian tilts his head, playing confused. "Ellie—"

"Don't call me that," I bite out. "That girl never existed, not in the way real people are supposed to exist."

Lola Otel's eyes widen. "Helena, dear—"

"No, Lola," I interrupt, my pulse hammering in my own ears. "They don't get to do this. Not anymore."

I look at Adrian, at his family, at the dining table laid out with glittering cutlery, untouched food, lavish displays of wealth. Everything that should have mattered to me. Everything that doesn't.

"You want to sit here and talk about the life I had?" I spit, my breath shallow. "The contracts, the parties, the dresses, the endless, exhausting performances? Do you think that's what matters? Do you think that's what made me whole?"

I take a step back from their table. "I left it all behind, Adrian. I left because I was dying."

The words land louder than any piece of expensive glass shattering on the Salvacions' marble floor.

I hear Beatriz breathe in sharply. Lolo Emil closes his eyes, his jaw tight. Lola's hands tremble as she grips her napkin. Even the Mayor regards me with narrowed eyes.

The only one who doesn't react is Adrian.

He simply stares at me.

I press on. "I didn't quit because I was tired or bored of it all. I didn't quit because I wanted to focus on my studies. I quit because I got sick."

My chest heaves but I don't stop.

I can't stop.

"Because I have Acute Myeloid Leukemia. Because I wake up every day knowing my body is failing me. Because I wanted to come home to my grandparents so I could die in peace."

I glance at my grandmother, at my grandfather. Their faces are drawn with leashed grief, with resignation and understanding. They knew this moment was coming.

Adrian looks around the table, as if flailing for someone to give an explanation, then turns his attention back to me. "Ellie, why didn't you—"

"Tell you?" I laugh, the sound pointed and bitter. "Because you wouldn't have listened."

He flinches.

I push on, merciless. "I came home because I wanted peace. I wanted to be surrounded by the people who actually love me, not by men who only see me as an accessory to their goddamn political ambitions."

I swallow back the lump in my throat, barely able to breathe past the weight of my own rage. "And now, even here, I can't have that peace, can I?"

Lola reaches for my arm. "Helena, *apo*, please—"

"You can have your wealth, Adrian," I continue, shaking my head. "You can have your cold, empty, pretentious little world. But you don't get to have me."

His expression darkens, something dangerous flashing in his eyes. But I don't care.

I'm done.

I'm done with him. With all of them.

I turn to Mayor Salvacion and his wife, drawing in a breath to steady myself. "Thank you for your hospitality, Mayor, Ma'am Beatriz. It was a lovely dinner." My voice is calm, almost eerily so.

Then I look at my stunned grandparents, my throat tightening. "Lolo, Lola, I'm so sorry. But I can't sit here and pretend anymore. I'll see you at home, okay?"

Then, with every ounce of dignity I have left, I turn on my heel and storm out of the room.

I don't turn back. I don't care about the gasps, the whispers, the opinions and judgment I leave behind.

I run.

Out of the house. Down the shiny stone steps.

Out into the night where I belong.

Where I know Tomas is waiting for me.

Chapter 30

The Immortal Heartbreak

TOMAS

The night around me settles like a hush, thick and unbroken.

I wait, leaning against the motorcycle, just beyond the reach of the streetlights outside the Salvacion estate. The air is heavy, the scent of the sea carried on the wind.

Overhead, the sky is darker than usual, the sliver of the moon barely visible.

New moon soon.

I should leave. If she does not come, I will know she has made her choice.

But then I hear footsteps—hurried, almost furious.

I turn and see Helena.

And I know.

She chose me.

She rushes toward me, breathless, her hair flying wild around her shoulders. She does not stop. She crashes into my chest, arms locking around my waist, pressing her face against me as if trying to bury herself in my skin.

I put my arms around her. Her body trembles, and I know it is not from the cold.

"Take me away," she says. "Please."

I do not ask her any questions. There is no need.

I knew she would come.

Without another word, I lift her onto the motorcycle, settling her behind me. Her arms wrap around my waist, her cheek presses against my back. She clings to me as if she is afraid I will disappear.

I rev the engine, and we melt into the night.

Instinct guides me. Not the road, not my mind, but something deeper.

I take her to the tree.

The *balete*.

The one from before.

The clearing is bathed in soft silver and gold, the fireflies returning as if they know. The tree stands tall, ancient, unmoving.

This is the same place where we first met, all those years ago.

Helena slides off the bike, staring at it in the sparse light.

I watch her, my chest tightening as her breathing becomes

unsteady.

"I remember this place," she whispers, her fingers grazing the trunk. "This is where…I don't know. But I feel it."

I swallow. "You do know."

She turns to me, her eyes searching mine. "Then tell me."

I close the distance between us. My hands find her waist, grounding myself in her warmth.

"I'm not who you think I am, Helena."

She does not pull away. She only waits.

I force the words out. "I was not born in this world. I was something else. Someone else. I was a warrior, a protector of my kind. I had no home, no family, no mate."

She shivers in my arms. "I remember you. Since I was seven. I don't know, but I feel it."

My heart clenches. "Yes."

She looks up at me, her voice breaking. "I always felt like something was missing. I couldn't explain it. But when I came back here, when I saw you…I knew. Not right away. But somehow—I did."

I hold her tighter, my forehead dropping against hers.

She remembers.

She *really* remembers now.

"The ember changed me," I continue, gesturing to the space in the middle of my chest. "By accident, it bound me to this world. It kept me here, even after the city took you from me. And when I felt your presence fading…" I choke on the words. "I didn't know why, but I changed. I became this. I was meant to be with you, even if all I could do was stay until the end."

She gasps, hands gripping my shoulders. "Don't say that."

"It's the truth, little one. And it's more than enough for me."

"No." Her voice is fierce, trembling. "No, Tomas. You weren't meant to just...stay. You were meant to be mine. I was meant to be yours. We were meant to be together."

Her fingers thread into my hair, tugging me down, and she presses her lips to mine.

Something inside me breaks.

I lift her, crushing her against me. Our mouths move frantically, as if we are trying to consume each other. She moans against me, and I moan back, feeling every inch of her.

She pulls at my shirt, and I strip it off, letting the night air wash over my skin. I kiss her again, harder, my hands roaming over her curves.

I need to remember everything.

Everything about her.

She pulls back only long enough to slip out of her dress.

"I want to stay with you," Helena says, her fingers grazing my chest. "Forever."

Then, finally, she says my name, so softly, so dreamily.

My true name.

"Magal-um."

I choke on my breath.

She knows.

I do not give her time to think. I lay her down on the forest floor, moving my body over hers, worshipping her with my hands, my mouth, my entire soul. I take my time. I kiss down her neck, over her breasts, down the softness of her stomach, until she is trembling beneath me, gasping my name.

I need her to feel it.

That this is not just love.

This is fate.

She arches into me, hands fisting in my hair, her body opening to me. And when I finally push into her, when I become one with her, I know it.

I feel it.

This is the only moment I will ever have.

I thrust deep, savoring every inch of her, every sound, every broken gasp. I take her again and again and again, until the world around us spins, until she is sobbing, until she is calling me—

Magal-um.

I lose myself.

Later, when we move to the stream, when I lift her in the water, when she sinks onto me beneath the star-strewn sky, I know tonight will be the last time.

But she does not.

She does not know that I will lose her. That the new moon will take me. That we will never have this again.

But my body knows.

For the first time in my life, I feel something I have never known before.

Tears slide down my face as I hold her close.

I do not understand what they mean in that moment, only that they belong to her.

Helena kisses them away, whispering, *I love you...I have always loved you...*

I close my eyes, my chest aching, my arms tightening around her.

And I answer.

I love you, little one. In this life—and in every life you shall live.

Chapter 31

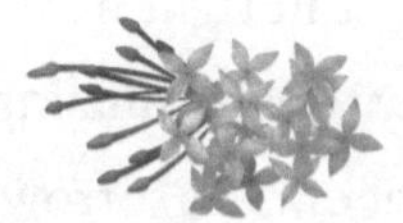

The Stolen Sunrise

HELENA

He is crying in my arms.

I have never seen him like this, never imagined that he was even capable of it.

His face is buried in my neck, his body trembling against mine, and his breaths come in ragged, shuddering waves. He doesn't make a sound, but I feel the depth of it.

"Tomas." I thread my fingers through his hair, damp with river water. "What is it? What's wrong?"

His grip tightens around me, pulling me closer, as if he's trying to fuse us together, as if holding me any tighter will keep me from slipping away. I wait, giving him time, letting him feel.

Finally, his lips part, his voice broken. "I don't know."

But I know he does.

His soul knows. Even his body does.

But I don't press him. I don't ask for an explanation he isn't ready to give. Instead, I lift his face, tracing the wetness on his cheeks with my thumbs. "I'm right here."

He closes his eyes at my touch, inhaling deeply. And then, just like that, something changes. The sorrow, the anguish—it burns away, replaced by something else.

Need.

Desperate, consuming need.

He brings his mouth against mine, his hands sliding up and down my back, tracing my waist and hips, branding every inch of me with his touch. We fall back onto the forest floor, tangled in sweat and moonlight, and he moves over me like a man starved.

"I don't want to stop," he breathes against my lips.

"Then don't," I answer, arching into him. "Please, don't."

We don't stop.

Not for hours. Not when the stars start to fade, not when the first hints of dawn creep over the horizon.

Not when my body trembles from exhaustion, not when my skin burns and blisters from the heat of his touch, not when my mind blurs between dream and reality.

Tomas moves over me like this night is all we will ever have. Like this is the only time he will ever get to touch me like this, love me like this.

And I let him.

I'm not afraid anymore. I have everything.

I have him.

And it is everything.

As we lay together, our bodies spent, our breaths mingling in the cool morning air, I say the words I've been too afraid to say.

"Tomas," I murmur, my fingers tracing the curve of his lips. "Maybe in your world, someday, we'll see each other again. Maybe we'll have our forever then."

His entire body stills. His arms around me tighten for just a second before he relaxes, pressing a soft kiss to my temple. He doesn't answer, but he doesn't have to. The way he holds me, the way he breathes me in, it is answer enough.

Then the sun rises.

The golden light spills over us, painting our skin in hues of fire and warmth, and I know. I feel it.

This is the last time.

I push him onto his back, straddling him, my hands splaying over his chest, feeling the steady, powerful beat of his heart. "One more time. Let me remember this."

He looks up at me, his eyes dark, burning, filled with something too vast for this world. He nods once.

So I take him. Deeply, completely. The way I want him to remember me. The way I want to remember him.

By the time we are done, the sun is high in the sky.

And we know.

It's over.

It has begun.

Tomas doesn't speak as he dresses me, as he helps me onto the motorcycle. But his hands linger, his fingers tracing my skin like he's engraving this moment onto his soul.

We ride in silence, the farm growing closer with each breath. My arms stay tight around him, clinging to his warmth, his strength, his love.

And it is enough.

It is everything.

Chapter 32

The Undying Stars

TOMAS

The sun is already high when we pull up to the farm gate.

The house is quiet, too quiet. But I know better. They have been waiting.

Helena slides off the bike first. There is no hesitation in her step as she walks up to the door, pushing it open.

Lola Otel and Lolo Emil are standing in the middle of the living room, their expressions weary and relieved.

Otel makes the first move. "Helena."

Helena rushes to her. She holds on tightly, as if she is a little girl again, tucking herself into her grandmother's arms. "I'm sorry for making you worry. But I won't apologize for what I said last night."

Emil sighs, stepping closer to hug her. "You don't have to, Helena." He looks at me then, and his eyes tell me everything. They knew. They knew I was out there, and they trusted me to bring her home. "We're just glad you're home, *apo*."

I look away as Emil and Otel hold her, as if they could somehow will their strength into her. Helena is saying something, her voice soft, thick with exhaustion, and I know she must be feeling the weight of everything.

The pretenses, the words, the truth. And yet, even as I stand apart, her presence reaches me. Her warmth, her heartbeat.

Otel turns her gaze to me. "Tomas."

I stiffen but meet her gaze. There is no judgment there. No anger.

Only sorrow. A kind of acceptance I do not want to acknowledge. Perhaps they pity me. Perhaps they know what this love means. What it will cost me.

"You brought her home," Emil says. "Thank you."

"There's no need to thank me, sir," I say, bowing my head slightly. "I'm only doing my duty."

Helena lifts her head at that, but I do not let myself meet her eyes. Not now.

"It will always be an honor to serve you," I continue.

My voice does not betray me, even if everything inside me is breaking into pieces.

Otel takes my hand. "You should have some breakfast. You must be hungry, out all night."

I shake my head. "It's fine, Lola. I'll be fine. Thank you."

I nod once more toward them, toward her, and turn away before the air suffocates me.

The moment I step outside, I inhale deeply. The scent of the fields, the morning air, the earth beneath my feet—these are the only things keeping me standing.

I walk.

I cross the fields toward my hut, enter, and shut the door behind me. My fingers find the wooden carving resting on the table, the one I have been working on for nearly a year.

It is of her.

Not as she is now, but as she was before.

Tiny, fearless, full of light.

The way I first saw her, when she was still running through the trees, her laughter catching in the wind. Before they took her away. Before they forced her to forget me.

I trace the lines of the carving, the delicate curve of her face, the tiny flowers woven into her hair.

I set the carving down, stretching my arms over my head. My body aches, but I welcome the pain. It keeps me grounded

I change out of last night's clothes, wash my face, drink water. And then I go outside to work.

The sun is higher now. The heat beats down on my skin, sweat sliding down my back, but I do not stop. If I stop moving, if I allow myself to think, I know it will be the end of me.

I take a breath, bending down to pull at the stubborn weeds near the mango grove. I do not look at the house.

I do not...but I feel it.

Her.

Her eyes watching me from her window. The weight of her

gaze presses into my back, into my chest, filling every hollow space inside me.

Slowly, I lift my head.

Our eyes meet.

Everything stills.

Her lips part, as if she is about to say something. I can see our night at the tree still clinging to her, the faint marks of my touch on her skin, the weight of the past lingering in her gaze.

For a moment, I want to go to her. I want to tell her it will be fine, that I will keep her safe, that nothing and no one can take her away from me.

But I do not.

I break the connection first.

I lower my eyes and return to my work.

Because I know the truth.

I have always known the truth.

So I say it, silently, in the heat of the sun, in the midmorning breeze, hoping she hears me.

Hoping she will know—and never forget.

I love you, Helena.

Then, now, until all the stars die.

Chapter 33

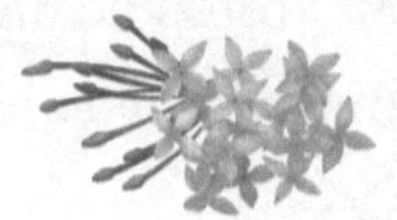

The Dreams of Innocence

HELENA

He doesn't look at me again.

I watch Tomas from my window, standing there in the sun, working the fields like nothing has changed. Like the world is the same. Like I'm the same.

But I'm not.

I press my forehead against the shutters. My body still hums with the weight of him, with the memory of his hands, his lips, his voice breaking against my skin.

The dress I wear is the same one from last night. The same one I had worn to the dinner with the Salvacions. But now it feels foreign, as though it no longer belongs to me. Because beneath the fabric, there is only him. His touch, his kisses, his mark on every inch of me.

I belong to him. Until my last breath and after it.

Tomas moves, his broad shoulders stretching against the morning sun as he bends down to gather crops, his hands steady. He looks as he always does, strong and unwavering, as if he could carry the weight of the entire world on his back and not falter.

But I know better.

I see the tension in the set of his jaw. The way his fingers hesitate, curling into the earth before he forces himself to keep going. I see the war in him, the way he wants to turn back, to look at me, to run to me and never stop.

But I know he won't.

He is letting me breathe. Letting me live.

I press my fingers to my chest, feeling the slow, steady rhythm beneath my skin. I wonder how long it will last.

I will live for him, I think.

As long as this body allows me, I will live for him.

I step away from the window. The world tilts slightly beneath my feet, the weight of exhaustion pulling at me. I need to sleep. I need to let my body recover.

The warm water soothes me as I bathe, washing away the remnants of the night, but not him. Never him. He is now in my blood, in my bones, in the very air I breathe.

And when I slip into bed, the world hazy around me, my last thought before sleep takes me is of him—of Magal-um, of his golden eyes, his hands upon me, his voice whispering my name in the language of the trees.

In my dreams, we are always together.

In my dreams, he reaches for me beneath the canopy of the ancient woods, his fingers tracing the curve of my face. His golden eyes shimmer like fireflies caught between the leaves, endless and knowing.

He gathers me against him, lifting me as effortlessly as he always had, my small hands pressed against the warmth of his chest, where I feel the steady, unfaltering rhythm of his heart. The same heart that has always beat for me.

He carries me through the whispering trees, where shadows dance and light flickers between the branches. Where the world is untouched, pure. Where we belong.

I thread *santan* flowers into his hair, laughing as he kneels so I can reach, my fingers tangling in the silk of it. He watches me with something reverent, something eternal in his eyes.

"Stay with me," I tell him, my hands slipping over his shoulders, my lips against the pulse of his throat. "Let me stay."

Magal-um cradles my face in his hands, his touch like a promise. *"In this world, little one, we will always be together."*

And I know—this is where I will stay. Here, in this dream, in this memory, in this love that has transcended time itself.

In my dreams, he will always be mine.

And I am always his.

Chapter 34

The Dark Descent

TOMAS

The day passes like an eternity.

Or a heartbeat.

I barely remember the moments in between—harvesting in the fields, my body moving automatically. I go through the motions, but my mind is elsewhere. Caught between the past and the inevitable.

Tomorrow is the night of the new moon.

I glance at the sky, the colors bleeding from gold to indigo. I strip off my shirt as I step into my hut, rolling my shoulders, willing the tension away. I pour cool water over myself, rinsing away the dirt and sweat of the day, but the ache inside me remains. I pull on a fresh shirt, steadying myself at the thought of seeing Helena at the house for dinner.

Then I hear voices.

The sound drifts from the gates.

Lolo Emil.

Clipped. Polite. Barely controlled.

And then another voice. Smooth, calculated, drenched in false charm.

Adrian Salvacion.

I freeze.

"We're grateful for your generosity, but Helena should be resting," Emil is saying. "Having you around will only upset her."

Adrian laughs, light and easy, but there is an edge beneath it. "Come on, Lolo. That's a bit harsh. I just wanted to check in. I brought flowers."

I wipe my face and step outside, following the voices.

I see them now.

Helena is on the porch with her grandmother, Lola Otel's frail arms wrapped around her. Otel is trembling, trying to keep Helena upright.

But it is Helena who looks Adrian straight in the eye, unflinching, even as the color drains from her face.

Emil stands firm, blocking Adrian's path. "Thank you for your concern, but Helena doesn't need visitors."

Adrian sighs, as if this is an inconvenience rather than a dismissal. He lifts the bouquet of roses, bright red, almost mocking. "I just wanted to apologize for last night. I didn't mean to insult anyone, not even him." He glances in my direction, barely. Contempt drips from his voice. "It was just a question. But if he can't answer it, that's not my fault."

Helena tenses.

Adrian keeps talking, his voice slick as oil. "Ellie, babe, I didn't know. I should have been looking after you. Please, let me talk to you."

She does not move.

Emil shakes his head. "Please leave, Adrian."

Adrian's smile tightens. "Come on, Lolo. Let's not make a scene."

Otel's voice wavers. "You should go, Adrian."

But Adrian pushes forward.

Pushes.

And Emil stumbles back, the old man's knees buckling as he hits the ground.

Otel screams.

Helena cries out, wrenching free from her grandmother to run to her grandfather. "Lolo!"

I do not think. I move.

Adrian barely has time to react before I slam into him, knocking him backward. He staggers, but I do not give him the chance to recover.

I hit him.

Hard.

His head jerks back with a sickening crack, his body twisting as he crumples to the ground.

But I do not stop.

I will not stop. Not this time.

I haul him up by his shirt and drive my fist into his ribs, feeling bone and muscle give way beneath my knuckles. He chokes, coughs, but I do not let him breathe.

I throw him to the dirt and drop onto him, straddling his chest. My fists come down—again, again, *again*—breaking skin, shattering arrogance. Blood spatters across the dirt, the scent thick and metallic.

He gasps, tries to shove me off, but he is weak.

Pathetic.

"YOU THINK YOU CAN TOUCH HER? YOU THINK YOU CAN PUSH THEM?"

Another punch. Another crunch.

Adrian's nose breaks, blood spilling down his face.

I cannot stop.

"YOU THINK YOUR MONEY, YOUR NAME, YOUR SO-CALLED POWER—ANY OF IT—MEANS ANYTHING?"

He does not answer.

He is choking on blood.

"Tomas!" Helena's voice cuts through the haze. I feel her hands on my arms, pulling, pleading. "Stop! Please!"

But I cannot.

Not after everything. Not after all the times I let this world take things from me. Take her from me.

Adrian's chest heaves. His lips part, swollen, bleeding, as he struggles for air. And then—

The glint of metal.

The gun appears from a holster beneath his polo shirt, shaking in his fingers, stained with his own blood. His eyes are wild, unfocused, but he points it at me, right between my ribs.

I finally stop.

The silence is deafening.

Adrian's breath rattles. He stumbles, barely able to stand, but he grins.

"Not so strong now, are you, Makalbang?"

My fists clench. I could still kill him. I should kill him.

But Helena...

I hear her breath hitch, see the terror in her eyes. Not for herself.

For me.

Adrian sways backward, spitting blood onto the dirt.

"This isn't over." His voice is hoarse, broken, but filled with malice. "Not ever."

Then he turns, staggering toward his truck, leaving a trail of red behind him.

I watch him go, every fiber of my being screaming to finish it.

But then Helena is in front of me, her hands shaking, her lips trembling as she reaches for me.

"Tomas," she whispers. "Come back."

I blink at the sight of her, then I look down.

The blood on my hands is warm. Adrian's blood. My own. It does not matter. None of it matters.

Except her.

I let out a slow, shaky breath and take her into my arms.

She is all that matters.

And all that ever will.

Chapter 35

The Bridge We Crossed

HELENA

I don't care about anything else.

Not Adrian, not what he's done, not what Tomas has done in return.

All I care about is that my grandfather is hurt, and Tomas might have killed Adrian.

I don't hesitate.

Tomas is in my arms, but his eyes have gone to a darker, angrier place. "It's okay. We're okay. We're all okay."

He doesn't move, doesn't respond, as I take his hands in mine. His skin feels cold, rigid. His chest heaves, his body still tense in the posture of a fighter ready to strike again. Adrian's blood is smeared across his knuckles, his forearms, staining his shirt. His breath is ragged, his shoulders rising and falling like he's trying to hold himself together, trying not to fall apart.

Behind me, Lola Otel sobs as she cradles my grandfather. Lolo Emil groans, rolling on the ground as he tries to get up.

He's alive. He's conscious.

I turn to Tomas, my hands cupping his face, forcing him to look at me.

"Tomas, we need to help Lolo. Please."

He looks at me like he's barely processing my words. Then his expression changes. Something in him clicks back into place.

Finally, he moves.

Without another word, Tomas lifts my grandfather into his arms. Lolo groans again, clutching at his side. Lola gasps, her hands fluttering over him in helpless panic.

"I'll take him inside," Tomas says.

None of us argue. He carries my grandfather into the house, laying him down gently on the living room sofa.

After making a quick call to Doctor Anas, I kneel next to them, taking Lolo's hand in mine. It's clammy and trembling. My grandmother hovers beside me, one arm around my shoulders, the other stroking my grandfather's head as she whispers prayers under her breath.

Tomas stands like a sentinel by the door, fists clenched at his sides. The sight of him like this—blood-soaked, protective, utterly terrifying—should unnerve me. It should make me afraid.

It doesn't.

But I don't want my grandparents to see him like this.

"Tomas," I say gently, "please go clean up before the doctor arrives."

He hesitates, then looks at me. Really looks at me.

Then he nods, slipping quietly out of the house.

As soon as he's gone, Lolo and Lola turn their attention to me.

Lola's hands shake as she brushes my hair back from my face. Lolo adjusts to a more upright position on the sofa with a pained grunt, but his eyes miss nothing.

"Tell me the truth, Helena," he says. "What's going on between you and that boy?"

I take a deep breath. There's no escaping this. Not anymore. I'm done hiding, done pretending.

"I love him, Lolo," I say simply.

Lola's breath catches.

Lolo blinks hard, his face unreadable.

"Since when?" he asks, his voice steady. "How long has this been happening?"

"Since the beginning," I answer softly. "Since I first saw him. Since before that, maybe."

Lola shakes her head, looking at us in turn. "We're not blind, *apo*. We've seen the way he looks at you. The way he's always looked at you. At your pictures, and when you got here..."

I swallow, my throat tight. "I know."

She sighs. "He's not just some farm boy, is he?"

I shake my head. "No."

She studies me, her wrinkled hands tightening around mine. "You don't even hesitate, do you? You say it like it's the simplest truth in the world."

I meet her gaze. "Because it is, Lola."

Lolo grunts. "That man will die for you, Helena."

"I know."

"He'll never leave you."

"I know."

Lolo looks at me, long and hard. "And you'll break his heart."

The words land like a knife to my chest. My grandmother makes a quiet sound, as if she wants to protest, but she knows it's true. We all do.

My voice wavers. "I don't want to."

"It doesn't matter what you want," my grandfather says gruffly. "It will happen anyway."

I look away, tears stinging my eyes.

Lola cups my face in her hands. "You deserve love, *apo*. You deserve someone who sees you for who you are. Someone who will never leave you."

I close my eyes. "I have him."

Silence.

Then Lolo mutters, "For now."

Tomas steps back into the house then, fresh and clean. His eyes dart between me and my grandparents, sensing the tension in the air. But I don't care.

I close the distance between us and, before I can second-guess myself, I throw my arms around him. He freezes, caught off guard, but then he wraps me in his arms, pressing me tightly against him.

No more hiding. No more secrets.

We have already crossed that bridge. There's no turning back now.

He holds me like he knows time is running out.

I hold him back like I refuse to let it.

The doctor arrives.

It's a bruised hip. Lolo will be fine, but he can't move around much in the next few days.

But outside, in the oncoming twilight, the fireflies are restless.

Chapter 36

The Magic of Her

TOMAS

The night stretches long before me.

And the fireflies draw closer.

Helena and I prepare dinner together. She is more tired than usual. I feel it in the way she moves, slower, as if every motion requires effort.

But she smiles, pretending for her grandparents, and I follow her lead.

The house is tense, the calm before the storm. No one wants to speak about what happened, but we must.

Over dinner, I lower my head and say, "I ask your forgiveness, sir, for not protecting you when you needed me. I should have been faster."

Lolo Emil chuckles, wincing slightly at the effort. "I would not have had a second thought if I were your age. I would have broken his nose too." He shakes his head, his voice laced with dry amusement. "That boy needed to be taken down from the pedestal he and his family put him on."

Helena watches me carefully, her fingers toying with the rim of her glass. She is worried for me, but she says nothing.

Emil sighs heavily. "Not that it matters much now. I'm not running for Barangay Councilor again next election. I'm too old for this. Maybe it's time your Lola and I finally travel. We've always wanted to see other parts of the Philippines. Maybe even the world."

Helena brightens at that. "That's a wonderful idea, Lolo! You'll love Thailand."

Lola Otel reaches over to pat her hand. "You both come with us. You and Tomas."

I force a smile, nodding. "That would be nice, Lola. I'd love to see a Muay Thai match in person."

"And the elephants," chimes in Helena. "They're so adorable. I got to meet some years ago. It would be nice to take proper pictures this time."

We all know that will never happen.

Otel sighs. "I hope Adrian learned his lesson. He was trespassing, after all."

Emil snorts. "They are Salvacions. They will see this however they want."

A shadow flickers across Helena's face. She grips my hand, her thumb brushing over my skinned knuckles.

"He might try to get back at you," she says quietly.

I squeeze her fingers. "I can handle Adrian Salvacion."

After dinner, I help Emil to bed while Otel fusses over him.

Helena lingers outside the house, arms wrapped around herself, waiting for me. When I step onto the porch, she looks up, the fireflies flitting around in the yard casting tiny, golden halos around her face.

She inclines her head, a small smile forming. "Would it be okay if I braid your hair?"

I stare at her. My chest tightens. It's what she used to do. The memories flood me—her little fingers weaving flowers into my hair, her laughter bright and unburdened.

The promise she made when she was ten.

I will come back.

And now, she has.

I sit on the steps. I watch Helena gather *santan* blossoms from the beds near the house. She threads the flowers carefully, then settles behind me and begins brushing my hair.

The air between us is thick with something unsaid, something only the fireflies know.

She does not speak for a long time, simply working, letting the night deepen around us.

At last, she says softly, "I missed doing this."

A lump rises in my throat. "I missed it too."

When she is done braiding, I hold out my arms.

She does not hesitate. She crawls into my lap, pressing her face against my chest, and I wrap my arms around her. She fits perfectly, as if she was made for this.

Made for me.

Her breath is warm against my skin. "Tell me a story."

I do. I tell her about my life before. About the old world.

I tell her about the ember, about the night I crossed the veil. About the first time I saw her. The little girl who held my hand without fear. About waiting for her after she left.

She listens, eyes heavy-lidded.

I take the wooden carving from my pocket—the figure of her I finally finished—and hold it out. "I spent almost a year trying to get this right...but something was always missing. I didn't realize what it was until you came home."

Her eyes glisten with unshed tears as her fingers trace the carving in my palm. She takes it from me, cradling it like something very precious. "It's beautiful."

I cup her face, brushing my thumb over her cheek. "You are beautiful."

She leans into my touch, closing her eyes. "Thank you. For everything. I never thought this kind of love existed, but it does. This is the magic I wanted."

I swallow hard. "You are my magic, Helena."

She smiles sleepily. "I love you, Magal-um."

My heart lurches—and, finally, breaks.

I hold her until she falls asleep against me, still clutching the wooden carving in her hands.

Then, slowly, I lift her and carry her inside the house. She stirs when I lay her on the bed, but she does not wake. Her breathing remains steady.

I sit in the chair by her window, watching the night give way to dawn.

Tonight is the new moon.

Chapter 37

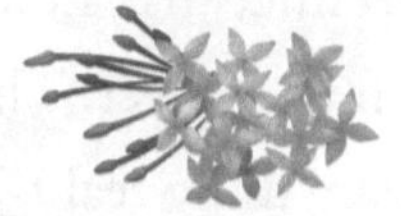

The Final Unraveling

HELENA

I wake up to the soft hum of conversation downstairs, the scent of Lola's cooking seeping through the wooden walls.

The house feels different today. The air feels like something is waiting, like the earth is holding its breath.

At lunch, my grandparents talk to me in gentle voices, asking how I slept, how I'm feeling. I answer without really thinking.

Tired. A little better. Hungry.

Tomas is nowhere near the table. He's been in and out all morning, but I haven't seen him eat. He only helps Lola move Lolo around, tending to him, working tirelessly like always.

When I step out onto the porch, I see him in the distance, working the farm like a man who can't afford to stop. Like stopping would break him.

I watch him for a long time, waiting for him to look up.

He never does.

Too tired to keep standing there, I go back inside. I call my parents, telling them I'm fine, that Lolo's injury isn't serious, that I'm doing what I can to recover. The conversation is short and stilted. We don't say anything real.

Afterward, I call Janine. She chatters about the university, her latest shopping trip, a new café that opened in the city. She says she misses me. I try to say it back, but my voice feels too small.

After the call, I scroll through my phone. My fingers hover over the first photo I took with Tomas. That day at the waiting shed. The first time I saw him. A selfie—me, smiling at the camera, and him, half-hidden in the frame, as if he never really belonged there.

It feels like a lifetime ago.

Maybe it was.

Doctor Anas arrives in the late afternoon to check on Lolo Emil and me. He tells me not to push myself too far, that I'm not responding to the medication like before. That something isn't right.

Tomas stands near the doorway, silent. Listening.

When the doctor leaves, Tomas walks him to the gate, murmuring quiet words of thanks. Lola Otel calls out, telling him to come in, to eat, to rest, but Tomas doesn't answer.

And that's when we hear it.

Engines.

I step onto the porch beside my grandparents.

Adrian's red truck is pulling up to the gate. There are three other cars with him. The kind of cars that don't belong here, that don't belong anywhere near this farm.

Men step out of the large, dark-colored SUVs.

All armed. Dangerous-looking. Nondescript.

But the man beside Adrian wears a police uniform. And the other—bespectacled, young, clean-cut—carries a medical bag.

Adrian limps to the front of his little battalion. His face is still swollen from Tomas' beating, but he's smiling.

"Good evening, Councilor Dosado, Ma'am Otel," he greets politely. "I'm very sorry to bother you, but we are placing Tomas Makalbang under arrest."

I don't feel my heart stop.

I feel nothing.

Adrian's voice is almost apologetic. "Not only for my assault, but for other crimes as well."

He reaches into his jacket, unfolding a piece of paper.

A police sketch.

A wanted poster.

Tomas.

Shorter hair, sharper lines, hollowed out, but undeniably him.

The name beneath it: *Damian Murillo.*

Adrian continues. "Did you know he was a runaway worker from a *hacienda* in Victorias City? That he killed his employer, stole from him, and went missing?" He glances at me, at my grandfather. "He's been hiding here all this time. And I have to wonder...did you know, Councilor?"

From beside me, I hear my grandfather take a shaky breath.

But I can't even move.

I look at Tomas. He doesn't flinch. He doesn't react. He just stands there.

Like he knew this moment was coming.

Lolo?

Tomas?

I try to say something, but no sound comes out of my throat. The world is narrowing, folding in on itself.

Adrian takes a few steps closer. "Ellie, babe...say something."

I can't.

I can't.

I stare at the poster. At the name I don't recognize.

At the face of the man I love.

It's not real.

None of this is real.

I don't want to believe anything. I refuse to believe anything.

No.

No.

Interlude 3

THE NEVER HEART

The sea is black under the new moon.

Wind lashes against my face as the boat groans, old and gasoline-powered, churning forward like it knows something I don't.

I don't even know where I'm going.

Just...away. Across the sea. To Iloilo.

I don't care.

Anywhere that isn't Victorias.

My hands are slick with blood. The wound in my side won't stop throbbing. It's deep. Rotten. The bandage I put over it hours ago is useless now, soaked through.

I don't remember how long I've been on the water. Time moves funny when your body's shutting down.

The only thing I do know? I'm not going back.

I close my eyes as the wind howls around me. My breath is shallow. Each inhale scrapes. Each exhale burns.

I just turned nineteen. The age you're supposed to begin your life—not end it.

It's all a fucking joke.

I used to work the sugar fields. Quietly, head down, always the first to arrive, always the last to leave. I never complained. Never asked for more than what I earned. Just gave them my back, my hands, my sweat. Every day. No questions.

Then the fevers began. At first I thought it was the heat. Or maybe just a curse of the fields, the kind you sleep off if you're lucky. But it didn't go away. It got worse.

The doctor in Bacolod said the word like it was a death sentence—*leukemia*—and suddenly, everything changed.

I started missing work. Not because I want to. Because I have to. Because the treatments took everything—time, strength, money I didn't have.

I had a chance to get better. The doctors said the chemo might work, if I stayed on the meds. If I rested. If I had money.

But the boss didn't care. Nobody did, if you're a faceless boy working the fields with nothing to your name.

One day late is a strike. Three days, and I'm as good as garbage.

I went back to collect the pay I earned. Three months of work, of blistered hands and broken skin. Not much. Enough for my pills. A few more tests. A little more time.

He laughed in my face. "You think you deserve anything?

You're already a corpse, Murillo."

I didn't plan to fight him. I swear I didn't. But something inside me snapped.

I don't remember grabbing the machete. I don't remember the shouting, or who struck first. All I remember is the crack of the gun, the fire in my gut, and a small pile of money I grabbed as I ran.

Not stolen. Earned. Mine.

I ran.

Through the cane fields. Through the back roads of Negros Occidental. For hours. Then days. I didn't sleep. I barely breathed. I bled, but I didn't stop.

Until I found the boat—small, battered, rocking gently at the edge of the dock like it's been waiting for me.

I took it.

Just like they took everything from me.

The sea doesn't welcome me. It claws at me. Tears into me. But I hold on.

And somehow, I make it.

I cough, and something wet and metallic fills my mouth. My ribs ache. My vision swims.

I see the lights of the coast. Could be Ajuy, maybe Concepcion.

I don't know.

The engine sputters once, then again, then dies completely.

The boat drifts. I clutch the edges and prepare for the crash.

When I hit the shore, I don't remember how I get out. All I know is the sand is soft under my knees, and the taste of salt is thick in my mouth. I haul myself up.

Step. Step. Another.

I'm running.

Through the mangroves. Through some tiny fishing village. I hear dogs bark, people talking, but I don't stop. I run like the blood leaking out of me doesn't matter. Like the bullet hasn't torn open half my stomach.

Like I still have time.

But I don't.

I stumble through trees. Climb up a hill. The path narrows. The stars spin.

Then I collapse.

The dirt is cold. The air is still. I fall against a great old tree, gnarled roots curling like fingers around me.

I blink up at the sky.

The moon isn't there.

Of course it isn't. It's the new moon.

I laugh. It hurts. A rattling, hollow sound.

My fingers twitch. I fumble in my pocket. Pull out the only thing that mattered enough to bring.

A newspaper clipping. Creased from folding and refolding, from months of being kept close and never let go.

A girl.

ELLIE DOSADO – 18 AND RADIANT, the headline read.

I'd seen it in the plantation office, a newspaper on someone's table, peeking from beneath some invoices. Just sitting there, like she was waiting for me. I stole it when no one was looking. Cut out her picture. Carried it with me every day. Didn't know why.

Just knew I wanted to.

She was beautiful. Not just the kind of pretty that makes boys dumb. The kind that makes you stop breathing.

The kind you dream about when you're lying in the dirt and you think maybe the world has something better waiting.

I never met her. Never would. But I kept the photo anyway.

"I guess I'll never meet you," I whisper to her, my voice barely audible.

I swallow. It feels like I'm swallowing glass.

"I bet you'd be so beautiful in person."

My fingers loosen.

The wind snatches the paper from my hand.

I watch it flutter upward, like it's being carried. Like it's going somewhere better.

The world is blurry now.

And then—

A flash.

Something darker than the night. A shadow that glides between the trees.

I try to focus.

But the last thing I see is the curve of that girl's face in my mind, smiling.

And then...nothing.

The last light inside me dies.

The dark falls silent.

And I never see her again.

Chapter 38

The New Moon

TOMAS

A memory slams into me.

Sharp. Rotten. Bleeding at the edges.

Black sea. No moon. Wind screaming against a stolen boat. A boy, barely a man, clutching his gut, blood pouring through his fingers. He is already dying, and he knows it.

Victorias fades behind him. Negros fades. But the pain does not.

He stumbles out of the sea and through the land, every step peeling him closer to the end. The world spins. His knees give. He collapses beneath an ancient tree.

His hand digs into his pocket.

A photograph. A creased newspaper clipping.

Ellie Dosado.

A stranger. A debutante. A girl from another world. One he was never meant to touch. An impossible longing.

His cracked lips twitch. A whisper through blood and breath.

I guess I'll never meet you.

The wind takes the paper from his hand.

And then—stillness.

But somewhere deep beneath the roots, something opens its eyes.

Now.

The present crashes down on me like a great weight.

I am Damian Murillo. I am Magal-um. I am Tomas Makalbang. I am all and none.

I stand surrounded.

Men. Guns. Adrian Salvacion, with his smug, broken face.

The farm is drowning in silence.

I do not resist. I lift my hands. I do not fight. I do not deny.

But before I step forward, I move to her.

Helena.

She is a statue of fury, of terror, of grief. Her hands tremble. Her breath is shallow, uneven, and yet she is not crying. Not yet.

I cup her face. Thumbs brush over her cheekbones, over her parted lips.

She breathes in, as if she is trying to memorize the scent of me.

"I love you, Heh-Leh-Nah."

Her body shakes. Her lips part, a whisper of a name.

"Tomas."

I kiss her, stealing her breath, giving her mine.

She sobs against me.

I turn away.

The fireflies leave.

The world turns cold.

Adrian's voice rings with triumph.

"My family has arranged everything. Doctor Fuentes here has been sent from Iloilo. He's here for Ellie."

A hush falls over the farm. A pause filled with unspeakable horror.

They are taking her.

Helena jerks, furious, screaming. "I'm of legal age! You can't take me! I make my own decisions!"

Otel clutches her as if she can hold her down.

Emil stumbles forward, pain in his every step.

"Your parents disagree," Adrian says. "They have signed off on your transfer."

The city doctor steps forward. Cold. Clinical. Unbothered.

"I have orders. She will receive treatment in Iloilo."

I move. I step between them and the gate.

I plant my feet. I straighten my spine. I block them all.

"Over my dead body," I say.

Adrian laughs. "That can be arranged."

And then—

All the lights go out.

The electricity. The streetlamps. The house. The cars.

All of it.

The new moon has come.

And with it, the dark.

The only light left is from the stars, from the sliver of a moonless sky that watches as the world begins to burn.

Gasps. Shuffling. The click of a gun.

"Check the breaker!" barks one of the Salvacion men, his voice laced with panic.

Adrian is silent.

But I hear him.

I hear them all. Their heartbeats. Their breaths.

I can smell their fear.

And I know, this is the moment.

I was never meant to be in chains.

I do not move at first. I stand still, waiting, watching, sensing.

The ground is damp beneath my feet. The air hums with the weight of something ancient, something unseen.

I can feel it. The ember. The bond. The fire inside me.

Helena is behind me, pressed against her grandmother, her grandfather just steps away. She is the only heartbeat I care about. The only life I would destroy the world to protect.

And yet, she is afraid. Not of them.

Of me.

I take a breath in.

I close my eyes.

And then I release it.

The power. The restraint. The humanity.

The lie.

The men around us go still.

They feel it now. They see it now.

A presence so massive, so overwhelming, so monstrous that it steals the breath from their lungs.

Their fingers tremble over triggers.

Adrian, battered, bruised, finally falters. When he speaks, his voice breaks. "What *the fuck* are you?"

I lift my head. I rise, to the trees, to the sky—and I let them see.

The darkness is my domain. It moves around me like a living thing, smoke rising from the smoldering coals of something not of this world.

The shadow of me spills beyond the farm, beyond the road, beyond what human eyes can comprehend.

A giant. A phantom. A nightmare made real.

My body does not change. My face does not change. But my essence, my nature, my truth begins to surface.

The fire inside me is no longer contained. It burns through my veins, branding me, branding them.

I know, in my bones, they will never forget. They will never unsee.

The city doctor is the first to panic. He stumbles back, muttering something under his breath. A prayer, a curse, a plea.

One of Adrian's men chokes. "W-what the fuck?"

Another raises his gun, but his hands shake too much to aim.

Adrian stands his ground, but I can smell it on him now, stronger.

Fear.

I step forward. One step.

They flinch.

Another.

They stumble back.

"Stop." Adrian's voice is hoarse, desperate. He lifts his gun.

But his hands are not steady. He is losing control.

Good.

A hand grasps my arm. Small. Warm.

I freeze.

Helena.

She is looking up at me. Her lips part. Her fingers clutch my skin.

And softly, so softly it almost breaks me, she says, "Magal-um...please."

And just like that, I am undone.

I stop.

The shadows recoil. The presence, the fire, the darkness, all of it withdraws.

I look at her. She looks right back at me.

And I know.

This is it.

This is goodbye.

Adrian senses the change. Like the coward he is, he takes advantage of it.

A flick of his wrist. The gun snaps up. A shot rings out.

The world stops.

And pain blossoms in my chest.

Chapter 39

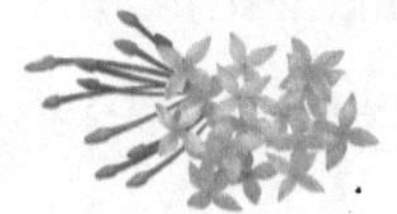

The Blackest Blood

HELENA

The gunshot rips through the night.

It shatters the stillness like a scream torn from the sky. Tomas does not feel it at first.

There's no moon. Just stars scattered like distant ash across the black sky. The night is deep, the kind that swallows everything whole.

And yet, I see him.

Not clearly. Not fully. But I see the shape of him. The curve of his shoulders tensing. The faint glint of sweat on his skin. The way his body jerks, not from surprise but from something more final.

The shadows don't hide him from me.

They never could.

Not when every breath between us is electric.

Not when I know him well enough to sense the wrongness before the sound even catches up.

He lurches forwards, like a string has snapped. His shoulders twist, spine arching. A sound tears from his throat—half a gasp, half a growl.

Then the blood comes. Not red.

Black. Thick. Shimmering. Alive.

It spills from the wound like ink, writhing under the starlight, moving like it has a will of its own. Like it's trying to crawl back inside him.

A scream claws out of my throat.

Not a cry. A raw, animal sound.

Then—

BOOM.

Another shot. From somewhere closer.

BOOM.

A third.

The bullets rain down like thunder, ripping through the trees, shredding the air.

He doesn't fall.

Then it ignites.

At first, it's just a flicker. Barely there, like heat lighting up beneath his skin. But then it pulses—a bright, primal gold.

A heartbeat made not of blood, but of fire and fury. It spreads in jagged paths across his chest and arms, like cracks in glass, like fault lines splitting him open from the inside out.

His veins glow. Lit from within, glowing through torn flesh and shadowed skin. The light pulses with a terrifying, hypnotic rhythm.

I don't know what it is. But I know it's not of this world.

The night recoils. The darkness itself seems to pull back from him. The air around him bends.

And for a second—just one breathless, impossible second—he glows.

Like a god awakened.

The stars above him seem dimmer. The world quieter.

I can't look away.

I watch as he raises his head. I watch as he, finally, moves.

Too fast. Too strong. Too furious.

The first man raises his rifle.

Too late.

Tomas grabs him by the collar and throws him straight into the side of Adrian's truck.

Metal crumples. Bones crack. The man doesn't move.

A second man points his gun at Tomas' temple, hands trembling.

But Tomas catches his wrist.

A twist. A sickening snap.

A scream.

The gun hits the dirt. So does the man.

The third thinks a knife will make a difference. A mistake.

Tomas grabs his face and slams it into the ground.

Once. Twice. Again.

Until there's only silence.

Then the fire comes.

From his hands. From his chest. From the place where that impossible light breaks through.

From the wrath of something never meant to be human.

It surges out of him—violent, furious, radiant.

It erupts. Not like a spark or flame, but like the ground itself is breathing out centuries of rage.

The grass ignites. The fence in front of the truck explodes.

The flames crawl fast, hungrily, as if they've been waiting.

The trees above us catch, but they don't burn down.

They burn up. Branches blaze like torches raised by forgotten gods, and for a moment, the night glows with something older than fire.

I should run. I should scream. But I can't move.

Because in the center of it all, Tomas stands.

Magal-um.

Damian.

Whatever or whoever he is now.

He turns and he faces Adrian.

The only one left. The one who thought he could control this. Who started all of this.

Adrian's bravado is gone.

His mask slips. His hands tremble like leaves in a storm. He stumbles back.

Tomas doesn't hesitate. He lunges.

Adrian trips, crashing into the side of his own truck. Smoke coils around them.

Tomas grabs him by the throat. Lifts him effortlessly. Like he weighs nothing. Slams him hard into the metal. The truck groans.

Adrian gasps, claws at the arm around his neck, his legs kicking wildly.

Tomas doesn't flinch. The light inside him burns brighter. It leaks through the cracks in his skin. Glows beneath his collarbones. Flares at the edges of his eyes until his face is cast in molten gold.

Adrian's mouth opens in a silent plea.

"YOU THINK YOU'RE POWERFUL?" Tomas growls.

The sound doesn't belong in this world. It echoes through the scorched night, through the burning world around us.

Something older speaks with him. Through him.

Something that doesn't forgive.

"YOU THINK YOU OWN HER?"

Adrian kicks, sputters. Tries to speak. He's no longer fighting—just flailing.

Tomas lifts him higher. *"I should end you."*

I know, with every cell in my body, that he means it.

Adrian's face twists, his eyes bulging, the veins in his throat rising against Tomas' grip.

Fire licks the truck. Flames curl up its sides. Metal glows red. Rubber warps.

The air tastes like ash and fury.

Adrian will burn with it.

But then a scream cuts through the night.

My scream.

I cry out his name. "Tomas!"

He hears me. In that second, with a world burning before him and death in his hands...

He still hears me.

His body stiffens.

He releases Adrian. Lets him fall like a broken puppet.

Adrian crashes to the dirt, choking, clawing at the earth, crawling away like the coward he is.

And Tomas staggers.

The light flickers.

He called it the ember. I remember that now.

The glow beneath his skin dims.

His shoulders slump. He sways, one step back. Then another...and falls.

I fall with him.

Pain bursts up my side. My knees slam into the ground. There's no strength left in them. Only cold. They crumple beneath me, and I drop hard into the dirt, hitting the ground with a jolt.

My hands scrape through ash and leaves and what's left of the world, grasping for something solid, but there is nothing left. Only soot and razed grass, the afterbirth of flame. The heat still pulses around us, erratic, but it's fading now. It's receding, like a tide that has finally given up on reaching the shore.

Then I feel it.

In my chest. In my ribs. The merciless unraveling of my body.

The fever returns like a wave.

The sickness—silent for days, held back by him, by his love, by something unearthly—surges forward now, unchained.

It claws up my spine. It drags needles through my veins. It wraps cold hands around my lungs and squeezes.

I can't breathe.

I can't breathe.

The night tilts. The stars spin. My mouth opens to scream, but no sound comes out—only a thin gasp, like something has been torn loose in my throat.

A firework of pain explodes in my chest.

Still I reach. I crawl.

I see shapes move in the firelight. Lola running. Lolo shouting, limping forward, his voice ragged and panicked.

None of it matters, because all I see is him.

Tomas.

Damian.

Magal-um.

He is on the ground now, glowing less, light fading fast. His arms are slack, splayed out like wings broken in flight.

His eyes are barely open, but they find me.

Even now.

Always now.

Always.

I drag myself to him until my palms settle on his chest. He's still pulsing softly with that light.

His strange-colored blood feels hot on my skin.

"Tomas." My voice cracks. I'm shaking.

He's trembling too.

My blood is ice now. My limbs are failing.

And I understand.

He's fading.

So am I.

Two dying things. Two broken lights.

Meeting at the edge of everything.

His hand finds mine in the dark. Clumsy, weakening, but still there. Our fingers lock.

I collapse onto his chest.

His heartbeat is fast. Too strong. Not human anymore.

His warmth seeps into me. He smells like the woods after lightning, like something forged in the deepest roots of the world.

"Stay with me," I plead. "Please, Tomas. Stay."

"Always, little one," he whispers back. "Always."

And then the world begins to fade.

But his arms are around me.

I know I will never fall alone.

Chapter 40

The Forever Tree

TOMAS

I cannot move.

Her breath falters against my skin.

She is slipping away.

I can hear Emil and Otel shouting, but the world is fading. The ember—my ember, our ember—is burning out. It is leaving me.

Helena is limp in my arms, her hand still tangled in mine, her fingers clutching my chest, over the place where my heart—Damian's heart—beats for her.

Only her.

The fire is dying.

The men are gone. The house is burning down. I feel the weight of the earth pressing down on me, calling me back.

I was never meant to be here. Not in this world. Not for long.

But she was here.

She was the light. She was the warmth. She was the heart of this world.

Now she is leaving it.

I try to speak. I try to tell her to stay, to fight, but the ember moves.

It is the last, dying breath of my soul.

And I understand.

It has burned for me long enough. It has burned through the void, through the veil, through the impossible binding of two souls that never should have met across realms.

The burden of it should have been mine to bear alone.

I should have left when I had the chance. I should have never held her.

I should have never loved her.

But I did.

And now...I will give her everything.

The ember ignites one last time.

A final sacrifice. A final wish.

A final light.

I press my hand to her chest, over her failing heart.

And I let go.

Suddenly, Helena gasps.

I can feel her lungs fill with breath. Her blood surges.

Her body—the one I protected, loved, and worshipped—seizes back to life.

And I, in turn, begin to fade.

The body I borrowed—Damian's body—weakens. My strength drains into her, into the girl I had waited for all my life, across the eternal skies.

My fire is hers now.

She is breathing.

She is alive.

While I am dying.

A smile curves my lips, the world blurring at the edges.

So I use what little strength I have left and pull her close. My arms are heavy now. Every movement feels like I am dragging my body through mud.

Because this is the last thing I will get to do.

Hold her.

This is what Damian wanted to do.

This is what Magal-um wants to do.

This is what Tomas will do now.

My hand slips into her hair. I press my lips to the crown of her head. Her scent—smoke, something sweet and a little wild—fills my senses.

I memorize it. I shall carry it wherever I go next.

Sky, sea, dust, fire. Eternity.

"You live, little one," I whisper into her hair. "I shall see you...in the stars."

Then the forever tree takes me in its shelter, one last time.

Chapter 41

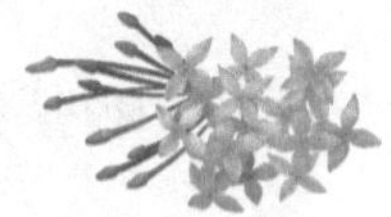

The Myth in My Heart

HELENA

I'm still on the ground.

Still clutching at nothing.

My hands tremble, fists clenched around air that no longer holds him. My nails are packed with ash and earth, and I dig deeper, desperate for something to anchor me. But there is nothing. Just scorched soil, still warm from a fire now extinguished.

The fireflies are gone.

Tomas is gone.

My chest is hollow, ripped wide open and left to bleed into the night.

There is no air in my lungs, just the echo of his heartbeat. The one I laid my ear against. The one I clung to. The one that is now, forever, still.

And yet the air moves.

A stirring. A wind too strong, too real, too alive, to be ordinary.

A shadow stretches beyond me, but I don't look up.

I don't care.

Let them come. Let them take me. Let them finish it. Let the world do what it wants. My war is over.

Then a voice cuts through the night.

Not loud, but vast. Like it came from below the earth or beyond the stars.

"You gave him happiness."

My body trembles.

It's not a comfort. It's not a kindness.

The voice keeps speaking, heavy in the unseen. *"You gave him something no world could ever give."*

I draw in a breath, but it's all wrong. Shaky. Thin. Like my ribs don't know how to hold grief this deep.

Behind me, I hear Lolo Emil groan.

Lola Otel is still weeping. Her cries break the air like pieces of glass.

But I can't move. I can't function. I can't even lift myself from the wreckage.

I am the wreckage.

Footsteps crunch over burned earth, drawing closer. Each step sounds like the beat of war drums, but somehow more peaceful, like a prelude to prayer.

I close my eyes.

"First Commander Magal-um only ever knew duty," the voice continues. *"In our world, he was legend. A warrior. A leader. A force even the gods revered. But in this world...he learned something else."*

A pause, followed by silence too deep, too knowing.

My body shakes. My fingers curl deeper into the dirt.

"He learned love."

With those words, my chest collapses inward. A gasp escapes me, raw and wet.

My body folds in on itself.

My arms wrap around where Tomas had been—where he'd held me, kissed me, chosen me.

"He fought for you," the voice says. *"He lived for you."*

A shape kneels beside me.

It moves slowly, carefully, but I can see it is too immense to be human.

I force my head up. Every muscle protests. Every inch of me aches.

He is towering. Cloaked in shadow. The kind of figure that belongs in ancient myth, not moonless nights.

But what strikes me most are his eyes. Glowing silver, calm as still water. They meet mine, and I see something there.

Loss.

Pride.

Grief.

He tilts his head.

"I thank you, Helena." His voice is like gravel and thunder. *"I*

thank you for giving my brother happiness."

My breath shatters, but I don't answer.

He turns to Lolo. To Lola.

"You cared for the First Commander in his last days," he says solemnly. *"You gave him a home when he had nothing. I honor you for that."*

Lolo, bruised and bent, still manages a nod.

Lola presses her hand to her mouth. Her shoulders shake. But she doesn't look away.

The shadow looks back to me. *"There was a time when he was feared more than any of us. He did not fall. He did not waver. He was the sword that struck first, the shield that never broke."*

My eyes burn. I can barely keep them open.

He glances at his own hands, large and scarred, as if remembering the weight of battle. His mouth hardens. *"He could have been anything. A king. A god. He could have ruled. Conquered. Destroyed."*

He falls silent, eyes locked on something far beyond the reach of the night around us.

"But in the end, he wanted only to be yours."

My heart splits wide open.

My sob escapes like a wound reopening. It tears from me with no warning, no mercy.

The shadow keeps speaking, softer now. A myth remembering a brother.

"I was there when he first earned his name. I saw him rise. I saw him break. I saw him kneel before the High Crown and offer his life a thousand times over. But I never saw him truly live...until he came here."

Another breath. A stillness.

He lifts his head to the sky.

To the stars. To where Tomas said he'd see me again.

"The ember is gone," the shadow says at last. His voice sounds more distant, more hollow. Not colder, just emptier. *"There is nothing left for me here."*

I go still.

Because I know what he means.

The ember.

It passed from Tomas, from Magal-um.

Into me.

I felt it. In the firelight. In the kiss. In the moment everything broke and remade itself around us.

I shake.

The shadow breathes out like he's made peace with something terrible, then he rises to his full height.

A mountain in motion.

"I bid you all farewell."

There is finality in it. A door closing between worlds.

The wind stirs once more. Wilder this time, but not cruel. Almost like it's carrying him.

Then he is gone.

Only the night remains.

Only me.

My hands sink into the blackened ground, heart in pieces.

Somewhere behind me, my grandparents are calling my name.

Somewhere, the world keeps turning.

But I stay there.

In the dirt.

In the ashes of a love I wasn't ready to lose.
Exactly where I belong.

Chapter 42

The Grave Garland

HELENA

The sea breeze smells like home.

It rustles through the trees, through the tall grass, through the narrow streets that weave between small houses and the quiet lives they hold.

I close my eyes for a moment, breathing it in, letting it settle inside me. It's the scent of salt and soil. Of rain about to fall. Of the life I almost lost, and the one I have decided to live.

Janine stands beside me, silent, giving me time. She has been patient. She has always been patient. Infinitely understanding beneath the force of her will, and unshakable in her devotion.

She insisted on coming to Concepcion to pick me up herself, no matter how much I told her I'd be fine. Her parents even arranged the car, made sure everything was perfect, like they were sending a daughter home instead of retrieving a friend.

We are standing in the little cemetery at the fringes of Barangay Santo Tomas.

The grave belongs to Damian Murillo.

A name I had never known.

An orphan boy who had run from Victorias, sick and dying, who had fought, who had tried to live. The chiseled letters look stark against the pale gray stone. Below them, a date—his birthdate. The same as mine.

I touch the stone, tracing the letters of his name.

I wonder if he had ever known, in his last breath, that he would become something else. That he would become someone else.

Janine watches me carefully. "Are you ready?"

I nod. "Yeah."

We step away and walk a little further.

To him.

The second grave is marked with a small gray headstone.

His grave.

There is no body. No birthdate. No epitaph.

No words to soften the finality of it.

Tomas Makalbang.

Just a name. A name that never belonged to him, but it was the only name that ever mattered.

A garland rests at the base of the marker. The *santan* flowers are already beginning to wilt, their bright orange petals curling inward, drinking the last of the air before they fade.

I reach into the plastic bag in my hand and pull out a fresh bundle of *santan*, tied with a white ribbon, a scrap from one of my dresses. The one he tore before he made love to me in his hut, a lifetime ago.

I kneel before the grave and place the flowers gently beside it.

I don't cry. I press my fingers into the earth.

"I'm here." The words come out soft, steady. "I made it, Magal-um."

The wind stirs, lifting the edges of my hair, cool against my skin.

Janine kneels beside me. I know what she wants to ask.

But she doesn't say it.

Instead, she leans in and puts an arm around my shoulders.

"It's time, Hel."

I swallow. Nod.

I take one last look at the grave, at the name that is both his and not his, at the marker that will never tell the whole story.

Then I rise to my feet. Janine follows, taking my hand in hers.

We walk back toward the road, where my grandparents are waiting.

Lola Otel and Lolo Emil stand with Manang Celia, the one they'll be staying with before they leave for their travels. A tricycle waits for them a short distance away, ready to whisk them away to the *poblacion*.

They deserve this. They have spent their whole lives taking care of others. Now, finally, they will take care of themselves.

Mayor Salvacion and Adrian's parents are paying for the repairs to the farm. An apology, but still a calculated move.

It doesn't erase what was done. It doesn't bring him back. But it is something.

Adrian has left town.

I don't ask where he is now.

I don't care.

My parents asked if they could come and pick me up. Their voices were careful, almost gentle, like they were afraid I might shatter if they pushed too hard.

I told them no. We'll meet back in the city, I said. We'll talk then. There's much to discuss.

Things that matter. Things we've avoided for too long.

But not today.

Today, the weight is too raw. The air too thick. The silence too loud.

Today is for ashes and earth, for things that can't be undone.

For grief I'm not yet ready to share.

So I told them to wait.

And they did.

I stop in front of my grandparents. The smile that touches my face is the first one I haven't had to force since the world ended.

"I love you," I say.

Lola wraps her arms around me, holding me tighter than she ever has. Her voice trembles with emotion. "You're always our beautiful girl, Helena."

Lolo presses a kiss to my forehead.

"Be good," he says, though his voice cracks halfway through. "Live well."

"We'll be visiting your Tia Carmela in Antique first," Lola adds. "Then a few other cousins in Capiz and Aklan. After that...Thailand, maybe."

"It's time we saw the world for ourselves," Lolo says, trying to smile.

I laugh softly, even as my throat tightens. "Thailand will love you both. Take lots of pictures for me, okay?"

Lola hands Janine a plastic container wrapped in a reusable bag. "Take care of our *apo*. And don't eat all the banana fritters at once."

"Legendary," Janine says, beaming. "Michelin-starred, Lola Otel. Thanks."

We all laugh. But beneath it, there is the heavy beat of farewell.

I thank Manang Celia for her kindness, and we say our goodbyes one last time—soft, lingering words that don't quite fill the emptiness that follows.

Then Janine and I step into the waiting car.

I turn back as we drive away, waving as Lola and Lolo grow smaller in the rearview mirror. The village of Santo Tomas begins to slip behind us, each winding turn of the road stealing away another familiar path, another corner of memory. The car hums gently beneath us, but my chest feels hollow.

As we pass the waiting shed, the one where I first met Tomas, I can't help it anymore.

I reach for Janine's hand and squeeze.

She tries to speak and hesitates, uncertain, the words caught somewhere between her lips and her thoughts. But then, at last, she lets them out.

"Your tests," she begins softly. "There's no sign of it anymore. No symptoms. No markers. Doctor Anas and Doctor Solis have gone over everything twice. And your blood work, Hel...it's clear. They said it's like you were never even sick."

I feel my throat lock up. My fingers clench around hers.

She shakes her head, still wide-eyed. "I mean...I still can't believe it. That it's all gone. That we're here. That you're here. It feels like a miracle."

A single tear slides down my cheek.

"Magic, Jan," I tell her with a smile. "I've always believed in it. And for once, it believed in me too."

I look out the window. At the road ahead. At the sky stretching open before us.

I breathe out slowly, then draw a breath back in. I shift my handbag slightly in my lap—and I smile again.

My fingers brush against the wooden carving of a little girl with flowers in her hair, safely tucked into the front pocket of my purse. She peeks out, smiling back at me.

No, she's laughing now.

She's ready to run into the forest to gather *datiles*.

"We're all meant to be where we are, when we are," I say.

Janine inclines her head. "You believe that?"

I nod. "I'm here, aren't I?"

She nudges me with her elbow. "And in a few weeks, you'll be at school. A midyear joiner." She shudders dramatically. "The agony."

I roll my eyes. "Don't remind me."

She grins. "Misery loves company, though. Someone else is joining midyear too."

I give her a sidelong glance. "Who?"

Janine winks. "You'll see."

I sigh, shaking my head. "I'm regretting this already."

She only laughs, giving me a quick embrace, along with a

playful little shake.

I let her.

As we drive farther away from the past and closer to what comes next, I think...

Maybe this is what Magal-um meant.

Maybe this is what it means to live.

Epilogue

THE ETERNAL TOUCH

The campus doesn't fit.

The halls are too bright. The voices too loud. The air too crisp.

Everything feels like a simulation. Too smooth, too whole. Like someone hit reset on the game, but I'm still carrying the data from a version that no longer exists.

I tighten my grip on my registration papers, all stamped and paid up after hours of queueing, the edges soft from how many times I've clutched and released them. They crinkle faintly in my hand, grounding me in something real. Something now.

Janine walks a half step ahead, practically buzzing with energy.

Her ponytail swings as she turns to speak, her tone light but insistent. "You're gonna do fine. It's just a semester late, not the end of the world."

I smile, because that's what I'm supposed to do. But it's the kind that pulls only at the surface, a reflex I've learned to perform. It doesn't reach my eyes.

Because the world already ended.

And I'm still learning how to live in its wreckage.

The quad is buzzing with life. People lying on the grass, laughing over coffee, backpacks slung over shoulders like no one's ever carried something heavier. Music drifts from a nearby wireless speaker. It all feels impossibly distant, like I'm watching through glass. Like I'm haunting a place I used to belong.

Janine doesn't seem to notice. Or maybe she does, but she's pretending for my sake.

"We're meeting him in the lounge," she says, slipping into her campus-queen tour-guide mode. "Just a quick hello. I think you'll like him."

Him.

I nod. I'm just following her steps, one foot in front of the other, like walking through fog.

The doors to the student lounge loom ahead—glass, steel, light. A world that kept moving while I stood still.

My stomach knots. Not with nerves, exactly, but an emptiness that still gapes wide open.

I know I'm here.

I'm alive.

And I'm trying.

But some days, that's all I can promise.

The lounge is filled with students, most likely new enrollees and transfers, some glancing around nervously, others glued to their phones.

Janine scans the room. Then she brightens. "Oh! There he is."

I barely hear her. "Who?"

She grins, tugging me along. "The other midyear joiner. Same major, same classes. He's nice, but..." She pauses, brows furrowing. "I dunno. Cute, but different."

I stare at her. "Different how?"

She shrugs. "You'll see. He's from Bacolod, so he's glad to have someone local around who's in the same boat. Figured you two could help each other settle in. Misery loves company, after all."

I can only shake my head resignedly. "Whatever you say, Jan. I'm just glad to be back with you."

She squeezes my hand with a smile and nods toward someone standing by the windows across the lounge. "That's him over there. International Taekwondo champion. His parents are in town for some real estate projects, but he's here to, you know, start over. Not sure if he's still competing, but..." She shrugs again. "Kind of a big deal."

I don't react. I can't.

Because my heart stops.

There's no mistaking him.

The build. The stance. The presence.

Exuding a quiet confidence that's impossible to ignore.

He's not dressed like the other guys. No preppy button-downs, no limited-edition shoes. Just a well-fitted black tee that clings to him in all the right places, sculpted to his chest and arms, highlighting the raw power underneath. The fabric falls just right, skimming his narrow hips with effortless grace. Cargo pants. Black sneakers.

Simple. Functional.

Familiar.

Like someone I once knew.

Like someone I once loved.

Then he turns.

And the world tilts.

Sunlight catches on his angular features, tracing over the lines of his jaw, the elegant curve of his lips—lips that once whispered my name, once pressed against my own. His skin is sun-kissed, rich and golden, like warmth I used to know.

Like warmth I still crave.

The hair is different, shorter and rough-cut, no longer wild but still untamed. His shoulders are broader, his frame even more powerful, his body built for speed and destruction. The kind of strength that makes bones break.

The kind of strength that once held me.

But it's his eyes.

A strange shade of brown.

Golden, in the right light.

The exact same.

Janine tugs me forward. "Helena, this is—"

"Grayson," he says.

It's his voice. As deep as when I first heard it over the phone, a lifetime ago.

Janine doesn't notice my reaction.

"Right!" she says brightly "Grayson Santisteban. He's in..."

Her voice fades.

Because he's looking at me.

Not just looking—watching. Studying. Waiting.

Janine's phone chimes. She looks at the screen impatiently.

"Shit, I have to go! I'll text you, okay? See you tomorrow, Hel. 'Bye, Grayson!"

And then she's gone.

It's just us.

The silence stretches.

Then he smiles knowingly.

My pulse slams into my ribs.

"Hey, little one."

No.

No.

No. No.

I feel it everywhere.

Like a ghost pressing against my skin.

Like a past that never died.

Like a love that will keep coming back to me.

He holds out his hand.

I don't think. I don't breathe. I just reach.

The moment our fingers touch—heat. Not warmth, not simple body heat, but something stronger.

A recognition. A pull. A storm surging beneath my skin.

Like the first time.

Like the first time I ever touched him.

His grip tightens just slightly, like he feels it too.

When he speaks, the world stills.

"You found me."

A breath leaves me, broken and trembling. My throat locks.

"I..." I can't speak.

Grayson cocks his head. "You're shaking."

"I'm not," I breathe out.

His smile softens. "Don't worry. I am too."

My hand burns. I swallow hard, trying to make sense of the moment, the past, the now. I grip my registration papers tighter.

"I—I've been here for two years," I say, trying to ground myself in the mundane. "But you...you'll have to be patient with my sense of direction. I still get lost in the buildings sometimes."

A flicker of something crosses his face.

A memory. A moment. A life once lived.

His hand is still wrapped around mine, thumb brushing absentmindedly along my skin.

"That's okay," he says. "I'll get lost with you."

Everything in me stills.

I can't breathe. I can't move.

Because I know.

I know those words.

I've heard them before.

In a forest bathed in fireflies.

Holding the hand of a boy—a man, a warrior—who was never meant to love me.

And yet, here he is.

My knees almost give out, but he holds me steady.

Like he always has.

Like he always will.

Love All Else

BOOKS IN THIS SERIES

Book One
Befallen

Coming soon...

Book Two
Begotten

About the Author

Shirley Siaton writes edgy and evocative novels and poems. Her worlds are in a deliciously dark cross-section of the romance, neo-noir, action, contemporary, and fantasy genres. Her background in various Asian martial arts inspires a lot of her work.

She has several books of fiction and poetry released since February 2023. Her first book is the free verse collection *Black Cat and other poems*. *Befallen* (March 2025) is her first full-length novel. She also pens juvenile literature as Shirley Parabia.

She is an award-winning writer, poet, and journalist in English, Filipino, and Hiligaynon. Her essays, short stories, and poems have been published internationally in print and digital media. Her multi-lingual plays have been staged in the Philippines.

Shirley is a black belt in Shotokan Karate and an international certified fitness coach. She has a Master's degree in Public Administration and works in education, wellness, and publishing. Originally from Iloilo City, she lives in the Middle East with her husband and two daughters.

On the Web

Shirley's official website: **shirleysiaton.com**

Complete reading guide: **shirley.pub**

Subscribe to Shirley's VIP list for free exclusive updates:
newsletter.shirleysiaton.com

www.ingramcontent.com/pod-product-compliance
Lightning Source LLC
Chambersburg PA
CBHW021036310726
48969CB00006B/1676